Rain Hare

Short Stories

Anna Barker

for Sandra, Lovely to meet you.
Very best wishes.
Anna.

IRON PRESS

First published 2022 by IRON Press
5 Marden Terrace
Cullercoats
North Shields
NE30 4PD
tel +44(0)191 2531901
ironpress@xlnmail.com
www.ironpress.co.uk
Find us on Facebook

ISBN 978-1-8383444-4-3
Printed by Imprint Digital

Cover and book design, Brian Grogan and Peter Mortimer
Typeset in Georgia 10pt

IRON Press books are distributed by
NBN International
and represented by Inpress Ltd
Milburn House, Dean Street
Newcastle upon Tyne NE1 1LF
tel: +44(0)191 2308104
www.inpressbooks.co.uk

Supported using public funding by
ARTS COUNCIL
ENGLAND
LOTTERY FUNDED

For Jessie

About the Author

ANNA BARKER (previously writing as Anna Ralph) is a journalist, novelist and poet. Her first novel, *The Floating Island* (Random House, 2007), won the Society of Authors' Betty Trask Award for best debut from a writer under 35. *Before I Knew Him* (Random House, 2008) was shortlisted for a Good Housekeeping Good Read award. As a journalist she won a Tom Cordner award and has written for *The Guardian*, *The Western Mail* and *The Journal*. In 2017 she obtained a PhD by Publication in Creative Writing from the University of Huddersfield. She is a Consultant Fellow with the Royal Literary Fund. Anna lives in Durham.

Acknowledgements

Thank you to David, Jessie and Pat who have been immensely supportive and patient while I wrote these stories. Marina Benjamin, Tina Pepler and Heather Dyer have cheered me on and encouraged my writing at various stages – your kindness has been invaluable. Many thanks to Peter Mortimer at IRON Press for steering these stories through to publication and putting up with my meddling! And finally, *Rain Hare* would not look so beautiful without the wonderful illustrations by Northumberland artist, Gillian Swaile, whose drawings feature on the inside pages of this book. Her immense talent has helped to bring the nature and landscapes of these stories to life. You can find more of Gillian's work at gillianswaileart.co.uk

The Stories

On the Flood

THERE ARE things I could do, things Dad would be telling me to do if he weren't six hours in the ground. I should fetch sandbags out of the garage, move furniture upstairs...but I'm tired and besides, the river is already here. I can't see it yet, but I can feel it and if I listen hard enough, past the sound of rain, I can hear its voice.

'Dad says if you listen to the river you hear all its echoes and stories, all of history for generations and generations.'

I think I knew she was there before she even spoke. I'd felt her moving through the house in the days leading up to the funeral, but she'd always leave a room just as I entered, leaving no trace of herself except the sense of something changed. She's taller than me, my fourteen-year-old self, which is a surprise, until I notice she's wearing those beat up Doc Martins I bought from the charity stall in town. They were a good buy, the finishing touch to my *fuck-you look*. The t-shirt I deliberately ripped at the shoulder is over the top, but I don't say so.

She glowers at me from behind a curtain of black fringe (not my natural colour). In a few months time she'll start backcombing it to make herself appear even taller. Probably around the time I'm into *The Cure*. I want to tell her she looks like the confidence I don't feel, never felt, as it turns out.

She slides on to one of the stools at the breakfast counter, drums her fingers, bitten down to nothing but painted black. Maybe I should offer her something to drink. Close the curtains? The river when it comes might frighten her and anyway, looking out every five minutes trying to work out if it's got closer isn't going to change anything.

'It's like that game,' she says.

'What game?'

She slides off the stool and starts opening cupboards, settles on some Ritz crackers she eats straight from the box. 'You know...the one where you say *what time is it?*'

'Mr Wolf.' *Can you read my mind?*

'Yeah, that one.'

It'd be a pretty sick twist if she could read my mind. It's bad enough she's here, in the house we've not lived in for thirty years. *I've* not lived in. This has to be one of those stress things. Or a breakdown, except people who are having a breakdown don't think 'I'm having a breakdown,' do they? They just get on with it. I look at her, one hand driven deep into the cracker box, the other fiddling with the headphones on her Walkman. This isn't even a good version of me. Fourteen was one of my worst years. The year I started seeing Dr Garth, I think, that dreadful woman who raved to Mum and Dad about behavioural activation therapy. *Do the things that make you happy and you'll be happy*, she kept saying.

The words are out of my mouth before I can stop them. 'What makes you happy?'

'I dunno.'

'Photography?'

No answer.

'Music?'

No answer.

'*The Cure*?'

'Who?'

Of course, it's the boy in sixth form who introduces her to them. Leo? No, Lenny, like Lenny Kravitz. I want to tell her to steer clear of him because he screws Suzie Chiang, but it feels like crossing a line. I pour myself another drink instead.

'Dad taught us his own version of Mr Wolf,' I say, emptying the last of Dad's whiskey (the 'every day' whiskey) into my glass. 'It was an ostrich instead of a wolf.'

'The wolf scared us. Ostrich was pretty terrifying too though.'

Does she know it was his funeral today? She doesn't seem upset, but then I'm not sure what upset would look like in this situation. I wish now I'd moved the boxes on the dining room table out to the car. They're full of his things. Oh God, the car. On the way back from the wake I saw a line of cars on the hill beside the war memorial, moved to higher ground. I should've been doing that sort of thing, not raking through boxes of the past, trying to make decisions about what to keep and what to get rid of. I expect I'll take it all up to the loft anyway as soon as I get home: my old schoolbooks and diaries, photo albums from holidays to Majorca and Lanzarote. Not all of it perhaps. Not the photo of Dad in his twenties on a field trip to Morocco I've not seen before, nor the one of the two of us on pebble island. Dad told me the island surfaced when the river was low, sometimes only for a few days. It'd been my idea to wade across to it. I'd pestered him until, in the end, probably fearing I'd attempt it alone, he bought waders and carried me across on his shoulders. In my memory I'd been older, but in the photo I look no more than six, maybe seven.

My fourteen-year-old self yawns. There's something fragile about this version of me, ephemeral, and I know without even asking her that the pain of being a teenager has pushed that day on the island with Dad – and how happy she was - to the furthest reaches of her mind.

'You could've had some cheese with those,' I say. 'There's brie in the fridge, I think.'

'I only like cheddar, the ones with mould make me vom.'

'Vom?'

'Vomit.'

'Brie doesn't have mould. You're thinking of blue cheese. Brie is white and creamy.'

She locks eyes with me, just a second, no more, of pure contempt that makes me want to congratulate her. This feels a bit like a continuation of those awkward conversations at the wake. People I didn't know or didn't remember knowing and who I'll never see again and so I made small talk about stuff that doesn't matter. Only that's not how I want this to be. I should have something pretty fucking important to say to my fourteen-year-old self, surely? I should impart some wisdom she'll actually benefit from, but I am me and my mind is blank. And she won't listen anyway.

'Is the river going to come into the house again?' She's looking at a box of books I packed up from Dad's study.

'No, it won't come that far.'

'I bet it's already in the garden, like it was when the chickens drowned.'

'They've put flood defences in since then. Once it stops raining the level will start to fall.'

She shrugs, fixes her stare somewhere to the left of my face like I'm the most boring person she's ever met. I want to say look, I've done all right, haven't I? Thanks to me, things are set fair for you and it's not like any of it came easy, you know. You think things are shit now, you're actually years away from rock bottom. But yes, the chickens were a blow and this flood will remind her of it. We didn't get them out in time even though I pleaded with Dad to let me bring them into the house. I even tried to sneak out when he was fetching sandbags, but he found me on the lawn, grabbed my arm, and pulled me back. I'd watched the coop float down the river from my bedroom window. She remembers it like it was a movie, my fourteen-year-old self, I can see it on her face, the mark it left. She catches my eye and looks away. Good for you, I think, you're already learning how to hide.

'I should probably get a few more things upstairs though,' I say. 'As a precaution.'

'As long as you're not planning on dumping it all in my room.'

Another drink. Not everyday whiskey, fuck it, this is not an everyday sort of day. I walk over to the cabinet and find the brandy I bought for Dad last Christmas, unopened. Next to it there's a bottle of vodka, years old judging by the label. There's a line drawn on the side in permanent green marker. It makes me laugh out loud. When did I start raiding the cabinet? Fifteen, surely? Not yet. I feel her eyes on my back and for a moment I'm tempted to offer her some, but I think better of it and gulp down the brandy before refilling.

'Are you getting drunk?'

'Yes.'

She gives me a weird kind of smile, like I did a dare. I smile back. Maybe we do get each other on some level. Maybe she's tougher than I give myself credit for and I've just forgotten how to access that part of myself. I want to tell her to come home after that wet November afternoon in 1998, when the leaves turn to ice on the patio and the sun makes a low arc across the sky, and Dad falls. I want to tell her to stay, that not everything is about her, and because art college doesn't work out anyway, and Dad needs you. But she's not going to be that person.

'You should read more books,' I say, hesitating over a third glass then pouring a smaller measure.

She looks at me in an 'oh my god, you're so lame' sort of way. 'I do read books. We're doing poetry at school.'

'What was that poem I liked? A Heaney poem.'

'All year the flax-dam festered in the heart of the townland; green and heavy headed.'

'Yes!' I point my finger, laugh, try to remember the next bit. 'Warm thick slobber of frogspawn that grew like clotted water.'

'That's not the next line.'

'Why do they do make you learn them by heart? It makes you stop loving them somehow.'

She slumps forward on the kitchen worktop, as though keeping herself upright, neck on top of shoulders, head on top of neck, is suddenly too much effort. If I didn't know her better, I'd think she was wilting from unending boredom of being me, but her lips are moving silently, reciting the poem under her breath. She catches my eye and presses her lips together.

'Do you still go to the wood over the metal footbridge?' I ask.

'Hoppers, yeah, sometimes. And before you say it, it isn't actually called Hoppers because of the frogs. It's got nothing to do with frogs.'

'There were tons of them though.'

In that pond we liked. We filled jam jars full of Heaney's thick slobber. I glance at her, hoping to see the same memory flash across her eyes, but I recognise nothing but the dark eyelashes she's already begun to pull out, a nervous habit she'll regret for years. I could tell her to stop or tell her which false eyelashes to buy that won't make her look permanently startled. I peer into the box from the study, hoping to find a book she'll like.

'Why don't you have any proper food?' she says. 'I'm starving.'

'Eels.'

'I meant pizza.'

'N-o. This. Eels.' I pull out a hardback, only now I have it in my hand,

I remember it's the one Dad gave me for my tenth birthday. He bookmarked several of the pages with strips of paper he tore from a copy of Reader's Digest. Oh, how I wish you won't know this grief.

'Are you crying?'

'Don't be silly.'

She gawps at me like I'm insane. I want to tell her she's wrong, how she ignores this book for years, yet she loves eels. She wants to know everything about them, but it's all here, right here in the book Dad gave her.

She wets a finger to dab at cracker crumbs on the kitchen counter, eats them.

'Please don't do that.'

'Why?'

'Because it's disgusting. And because it's rude when I'm trying to tell you something, something important about this book. 'Here,' I hold it out for her. 'You'll like it.'

'I've read it.'

'Have you though?'

She lowers her head to the counter, sticks out her tongue, and licks up the crumbs, her eyes locked on mine. My God, she's good. It takes enormous talent to be that insolent. She needs to learn when to use it to its best effect though. I don't think I ever do, not really. I walk over to the patio window. It's almost dusk, the day swinging on its hinge. I can barely make out the shapes of the firs at the bottom of the garden now, but I can see they're swaying, which is odd because until now it's just been rain, rain, more bloody rain. But not wind. Wind is new. Perhaps all this will blow itself out.

I drain my glass. I should've brought home the left-over wine from the wake. It's obvious this is going to be a long night and though I don't want to admit it, I'm afraid of the river. I know it comes slowly, creeping, I know it doesn't come in a great rush and yet I fear that's exactly what it'll do. A giant wave that knocks the air out of our lungs and we won't have time to say anything really important. I look at her, so grown up and yet so young. So naïve. Don't wear the short skirt to the job interview at Nissan. Don't have sex with Tom on the night of your 21st birthday because he'll steal the contents of your flat to buy drugs. Don't regret cutting your hair short because despite what your so-called friends will say, you'll never look more beautiful. Know yourself, find *something* in yourself, *anything*, to love. Fuck what other people think.

She isn't looking at the book. She's pushed it away along the kitchen counter and is instead spinning her Walkman round and round. She sighs deeply then gets up and comes to stand with me at the window. I wonder if she's afraid, if she is, she's doing a good job of not showing it. I feel her hand touch mine, gently lifting it up and, as she lifts it, she blows a hot breath onto the glass. With the tip of my finger I write our name.

'They come from the Sargasso Sea,' she says, after a long silence. 'Swim up the river, thousands of them, they hide in the mud.'

'Elvers.'

'That's what I meant. Elvers.'

'So you did read the book.'

'Elvers is a stupid name for baby eels. They should be called eelies, or something.'

'Baby elves should be called elvers...'

'I know, right?' She laughs and for a second I'm so overcome with love for her I want to reach out and rest my hand on the top of her head, the way a mother might, but the moment passes.

She cups her hands around her eyes and leans into the patio window to look out over the garden. 'Do you think they're out there now? In the storm, trying to get home to the Sargasso Sea? I don't see a moon.'

It hasn't occurred to me but it's entirely possible. Right time of year, no moon, a storm big enough to wake them from the mud. The man Dad called Tedry sold smoked eel from a shack on the river, maybe a mile from here, though it'll be long gone now. He kept live ones in barrels with chicken wire lids to stop them escaping. If I close my eyes, I can still see the eels, and what became of them: the racks, how he strung them up high along the length of the roof, row after row of eels, hung from their heads, slit down their lengths. Tedry was the one who told me about the eel migration. He crouched down until he was level with my eyes and I could smell his tobacco and woodsmoke on his wax jacket and he'd tell me how all year the eels hid in the fat of the river mud, half-buried, slack mouthed, one eye open to watch the moon. *New moon, half moon, full moon, no moon.* He said it like that, over and over, like it was a nursery rhyme. Only when there was no moon to see in the sky did the eels wake and start their journey home, dozens of them, slick and silvered princes.

My fourteen-year-old self shivers, rubs the length of her arms with her hands. 'They never got home, did they? The eels Tedry caught?'

'No.'

'Mr Lupton says it might be like they're following the magnetic pull of the earth or something.'

'Biology teacher, right? Christ. Too late to tell you not to write about him in your diary. Mum and Dad will read them all when you leave home.'

'Why would you say that?! No, they won't. You're lying.' She's blushing, her eyes night black.

Shit. Of course she doesn't want me to know how she crushed on him for years, yet of course I know! A crush, Jesus, it's beautiful, yes, but private, even from me. Now I'm filled with the panic of her leaving, I can't even manage not to ruin this. I try and remember something else to say about eels, to get us back to where we were.

'Do you think it's true about their eyes, them changing from brown to blue when they migrate?'

'How should I know?' She turns away from the window and slumps into Dad's old office chair, lightly tapping the arms just as he used to. She has his hands, long piano perfect fingers. I have his hands.

'I think they do,' I say. 'At least, I like to think they do.'

'It's just something people say to make them sound magical.'

'They are magical.'

She shrugs. When did I let that wonder escape? I want a year, a day, a moment I can pinpoint when it leaves. I used to be full of such curiosity. University will bleed it out of her, that's for sure, but not now, not yet. That's the thing, you sweet fucked up child, you have to stay curious, don't always be so quick to doubt yourself. To settle. You've got ideas, passions. You wanted to be a scientist, once.

'What's that noise?' she says, leaning forward in the chair.

I hear it too. It's coming from behind the door of the utility room. Nervously, I open it, stepping back sharply when I see that the river has started to come in through the cat flap, sloshing in waves and covering the tiled floor in an inch of muddy brown.

'We should go upstairs,' I say, smiling to soften the panic I hear in my voice.

The smallest flicker of fear moves like a shadow across her face before she stands up and fetches her Walkman off the kitchen counter, wrapping the headphone wire round and round. 'Shall I take one of these boxes?'

It moves me, how she masks that fear. You'll be all right, I think, more than all right. Won't she? I'm not all right. I'm alone. There was no one to bring with me to the funeral, no one to help do all this. I've pushed them away. Don't do that, you need people to remind you who you are.

Once we're in the bedroom we sit with the main light on, me on the bed, her on the beanbag in the corner of the room. It's more her room than mine. I didn't even sleep in it when I came to see Dad and coming back for the funeral, I did what I always do, without thinking, and made up the sofa bed. The light flickers several times before settling. The power will go off soon. Why didn't I think of that when we were still downstairs? I'm not prepared. I'm not thinking at all. Now I'll have to go back and get candles, find matches.

'Will you be all right for a minute?'

She's put her headphones on and so doesn't hear me. I go quickly, pausing at the wooden chest on the landing to pull out extra blankets. What else? I don't know. It all seems so stupid when I could just leave, at any moment I could just grab my keys and get out, chance the roads being clear but I've already talked myself past that point. If the roads weren't flooded before they will be now, or trees will be down, their roots softened by water.

When I get to the kitchen, I see that the river has already reached the breakfast bar. It glistens, like something living. Dad's slippers are floating in it like two weathered boats. I breathe in the smell of river silt, the rot of it, the sharp shock of the past. *Echoes and stories, all of history for generations and generations.* I take a deep breath, yank off my socks and stuff them into the pockets of my cardigan and then splash through the icy cold water, first trying the dresser for candles and then remembering Dad would've kept them in the utility room. I find a single fat white candle and matches in one of the drawers next to his tools and race back upstairs.

She hasn't moved except for closing her eyes. Her lips mouth the words to a song I can't hear. This is what I did when I was frightened. When Mum and Dad fought late into the night, when the thought of school the next day made the blood in my ears feel hot. I drop one of the blankets onto the floor beside her and then sit with my knees pulled up to my chest on the window seat, a habit I can tell she recognises when she opens her eyes to find me there. I smile, hoping she'll want to talk some more but she looks away, artfully dodging me in that beautiful way of hers.

I look outside, into the dark. The wind has died down, the tops of the firs barely moving. The glass on the window is flecked with rain, but that too seems to have slowed at least. In its place there's a stillness, more frightening somehow. I don't know whether it's because we're in the eye of the storm, or because the river rolls beneath us now, but I am afraid. Fourteen-year-old self stands up and without saying a word, she joins me on the window seat. Together, we listen to the sound of the house, of the river *in* the house, the knocks, things being lifted up and shoved against walls. I look for the moon, crane my neck to search every part of the visible sky as though the moon itself might offer an escape, but it's just black, there aren't even any stars.

Some hours later, or perhaps only minutes, I wake to the sound of the phone ringing, but it stops and I'm not sure whether I heard it, or it was a dream. Outside, it's started to get light, barely yet dawn, but light enough to make out shapes in the garden below. Strange, changed, though it's not clear at first what's different. The river still stretches over the lawn, all the way to the patio but no longer covering it as it did last night. In its wake it's left a thick dark brown sludge and a tide mark on the patio window several feet high.

'I think it's over,' I say, but she's not beside me, or on the beanbag, or on the bed.

I get down from the window seat and go out onto the landing, shouting my own name.

No answer.

I press a hand to my temple, feel a swell of nausea rise in the back of my throat. What am I doing? I know, of course I know, she's gone. Of course, I know, in the part of myself I keep hidden, that she was never really here. And yet I look for her in every room: in Dad's bedroom where his suit jacket still hangs on the bedroom chair in the shape of him; in the loft where once I made a secret den full of books; in the garage where to my surprise I find the chicken coop I saw float away, years ago.

It's hard to admit she's gone. All that remains now are the marks left by the river. In the kitchen a saucepan lies upturned on the floor and beside the patio window there's a flotsam tide line. It isn't until I get closer that I see the door is ajar, forced open by the river, the glass cracked in one corner. Outside, the garden is littered: a wrecked shopping trolley, a barbie doll, an empty whiskey bottle, an old gardening cap of Dad's, a slow cooker, and furthest away, right where the garden meets the path to the river, there's a book. *The Book of Eels: Their Lives, Secrets, and Myths.* The slips of paper Dad used as bookmarks are gone and pages are stuck together with the river's dark silt, but I can save it, it's not a lost cause. I can make it all right. Some things are worth saving.

How Do I Feel About Lentils?

THE BOY'S in the hide. Seen him a couple of times now with his camera. Nice lad. I try to summon his name. It's there, at the edges. Reminds me of Phillip at that age, lanky, feet a bit too big for him, like a Moorhen chick. He'll grow into them. What's his *name*? No, won't come. Should've written it down.

'All right,' he says.

'Now then. How's it looking?'

'You just missed an Avocet.'

'*Never.* You get a photo?'

'Yeah, but it's not great.'

I peer over his shoulder while he searches for it in his camera. Got a good eye, great shot of a Sandpiper. 'That's a belter, that one.'

'Yeah, got lucky. I was up near Emmanuel Point, you know where it shelves down and then there's a drop?'

I try to think where he means, but nothing comes. 'Aye, I know it.'

He finds the Avocet. 'Composition's okay, but I didn't get the eye in focus.'

'No, get the eye and you've got the shot, doesn't matter if the feathers are a bit out, as long as you get the eye.'

He nods. Maybe I told him that before. I set up further along the bench. The window's down. I try to raise it, but it won't clip in. He sees me struggling and comes over, easily dropping the catch.

'They're a bit stiff,' he says.

Nice lad. His nails are bitten to the quick, dirt ground into the cuticles. Phillip planting tulip bulbs in the tub on the patio. I see us there, side-by-side, me kneeling on a cushion. I'm handing him the bulbs, telling him how deep to make the hole. Years ago. Before we fell out, though what we fell out about God alone knows. I did know, once. Must've. I try to recall my last conversation with him, but it's just an image, his face full of anger, no words.

'Thank you, Phillip.'

'Toby.'

'Ah, yes, so it is.'

He gives me a shy sideways smile and returns to his spot on the bench.

'You enjoying your holiday then?'

He shrugs. 'Yeah, I guess. Told me mates I was going to New York.'

'I went to Montana once, had an uncle lived there. New York, eh?'

'If they knew I was going birding they wouldn't half take the piss.'

He looks through his camera, focuses on something I can't see, takes a shot.

'Tell 'em you've seen a Pallus Warbler, that'll shut them up.'

'A what...?'

'Two sightings in forty years. That's in the whole of the UK, mind.'

He smiles, shakes his head.

For a minute or two we look out over the pond, a silence settling between us. Been birding on my own for so long I've forgotten what it's like to have company, though this lad's quieter than Tommy. By heck, Tommy, we had some crack when we went birding. Not thought of him for years. Killed in action on that bloody beach, first day, was it? Or was it the second? He'd have been what, nineteen. Not that much older than this lad.

He's spotted something. A grebe? Haven't got my binoculars out yet.

'So why would they take the piss then? Your mates?'

He puts down his camera. Maybe I'm a bother and should leave him be, but then he says: 'Birding just isn't cool, you know. I mean, for someone my age. Ok, if you're...'

'Old?'

He rubs his nose.

'Oh, don't worry yourself, lad. I'm eighty-three, that's plenty old. Here,' I offer him one of the pasties Mary fetched from the bakers. 'Get your mits round that.'

'Thanks.'

'Me and this mate of mine, Tommy Pigeon, we'd go out every weekend birding when we were your age. We had a book, bit like the one you've got there.'

'He wasn't called Tommy Pigeon though, was he?'

'He wasn't? I don't know, you might be right.'

'No, I mean, *pigeon*.'

'Oh, I see.' Yes, I remember now, it was a thing him having a name like that. 'No, definitely Pigeon. Girls loved him, real charmer. Wasn't for Tommy I wouldn't have met Mary.'

'How come?'

'There was this girl Tommy fancied, Kathy or Kate, something like that, anyway he gets her and her friend, Mary, to come birding with us.'

'What, like a *date*?'

'Suppose it was. First date. You got a girl?'

'Be serious.' He looks away, flicks bits of pastry off his jeans.

'Why not? Nowt wrong with you.' Shy, mind. Suppose I was no different. 'Well, you want a girl, you take her birding.'

'Not the lasses at my school, they'd sooner stick pins in their eyes.'

'Best place for a date, a hide.'

'Yeah?'

'Oh, go on, use your imagination.'

'Ah man! No way, did you just wink?' He laughs then, proper belly laugh. 'You're glass, man, pure glass.'

Class, I think he says, sounded like glass, but I'm not sure what being glass would be about. Talk funny kids these days, but then there was that thing Phillip used to say...Square, that's right. Everything was square.

'You been married a long time then, you and... Mary?'

'Sixty-one years, or it could be sixty-four. She'd tell you.'

He sucks in a breath. 'That's ages.'

'Yep.'

'Won't she be mad at you for not remembering?'

'Got a get out of jail free card.' I tap the side of my head. 'Don't remember stuff like I used to.'

'You remembered Tommy Pigeon.'

'So I did.' Funny, I don't often tell people about me forgetting things, but somehow I don't mind telling this kid. Maybe it's easier to be old around the young. 'I got a trick up my sleeve though, see?' I open my logbook at random. 'I write stuff down, used to just be a record of birds, but now...what does that say..?'

He slides over, tries to read my handwriting. 'Time, and date, I think.'

'No, not there, this extra column.' I slip my specs on, read from the top. 'There, you see? Mary's birthday. Warfarin clinic, 2.15. Put the bins out. It's like a trail of breadcrumbs I lay for myself.'

He points to an entry on the opposite page. 'An Eastern Black Redstart? Always wanted to see one of them.'

'Ah yes, now when was that?'

'You've written it down, look, May 11th, 2002.'

'Drove two hundred miles for that fella, I did.' I laugh, startled at my memory of it, clear as the day I wrote it down. 'Wouldn't think twice about driving two hundred miles then, mad, though, isn't it, when you come to think of it? Just on the off chance you might get a glimpse.'

'I dunno, I think it's pretty cool. You got one you're still after?'

I close the book. 'Aye, maybe.'

'Can I guess?'

'Go on then.'

'Osprey?'

'Bigger.'

'What's bigger?' He looks confused. 'Golden Eagle?'

'A migration.'

'Yeah, but that's not one bird.'

'Thousands, not all at once, of course, but there's usually one night when there's so many of them they almost fill the sky. Here, Sandham Cove?'

He nods.

'Or at least I suppose they do. Donkey's years I've been coming here and I've still not seen it.'

'But doesn't it happen every year?'

'Aye, but when, which night?' A memory of Tommy hunkered down in the shadow of a dune. 'I suppose you might say it's my holy grail.

You'll have yours, too, I expect.'

He looks out over the pond. 'I just like taking pictures.'

'You better get some more then.'

He shuffles back over to his spot, but we don't chat much after that until he's ready to move on to his next pitch. 'Might have a look round Sandham Cove,' he says. I watch him from the hide window, waving when he looks back, then I see him cross the open fields on to the reserve.

I hang around a bit, but I don't settle. The hide has a different quality, changed by his presence, emptier now he's gone. I look out, just a few ducks anyhow. They're a jittery lot, a change of mood sees them bluster across the water, rise as one with a great clack and then skid into the reed stalks. Maybe a fox about. I pack up, feeling tired, the walk back suddenly a chore.

Outside it's got colder, the fields gripped by frost. Better get a move on, Mary'll be getting worried. I check my hand-clock. Funny slip, that one. I said it to her last week, the word 'watch' just wouldn't come. We laughed about it. Now, of course, we'll call it a hand-clock all the time. At least we can still laugh.

Tide's out I see, oystercatchers have gathered on the ribbed sand in their usual state of constant vigilance, hair trigger responses to dangers unseen, but felt. I tug my hat down over my ears and put my head into the wind. It's a challenge to walk in it, gusts from every which way, but mostly it blows straight off the sea and I have to pit my weight against it. Funny thinking of Tommy like that, out of the blue. Always young, Tommy, and Phillip, always angry. Their faces are a blur though, like I'm looking at them through mist.

Mary doesn't get angry - as well she might - but I hear the note of strained patience in her voice sometimes. We're not going to let it spoil things, she says. But there's stuff I don't tell her about, how once, or maybe twice, I've woken in the night, seen her beside me and not known her. It'd hurt her, that. Such nonsense anyway. Like coming to out of a dream, that's all it is, seconds only, gone the moment I curl into her back, get her smell.

As I reach the familiar line of grave oak trees I look up to their branches. Last year's dry leaves are shivering out notes. That's it, that's the weird thing about it, I see those leaves and immediately I think 'oak', and yet I couldn't get 'watch.' I look around me, fixing on all the other things I can name as well today as I could yesterday: tight buds on the hawthorn, nipped-looking crocuses dotting the grass verge, a scab of yellow-crusted lichen on the wall.

That's the trick, Mary says. As long as I don't stray from what's familiar, I can choose a single moment and be right in it, my mind will stay there with me. I can keep it whole.

We eat early in the restaurant; dusk falling on the garden. The boy's at a table with his parents, he gives me a timid nod as I pass, but I don't stop, don't want to embarrass the lad. Mary chooses a spot by the window. I see a mistle thrush high on a branch in the apple tree, feathers ruffled by the wind, singing his heart out the way they do when there's a storm coming. Storm-cock. Aye, that's his other name.

'Are you hungry?' Mary says.

'I could eat a horse.'

'Didn't you have your pasties?'

'Gave one to the lad.' I nod in his direction. He's on his phone, his parents deep in conversation. 'Saw him in the hide today.'

I want to ask her why Phillip's angry, but I know it'll upset her, and she's made a bit of an effort, got her nice necklace on and her blue dress. It'll come to me. I put my specs on to look at the menu, but it's the same as last night. Cottage pie, sea bass. Lentil curry.

'How do I feel about lentils?' I ask her.

'You like them.'

Play havoc with me insides, mind, but I need something to perk me up or I'll be nodding off before Mary gets her pudding. As it is, she skips it and we move into the bar, Mary with her half lager and me with my Guinness. We're playing pontoon for pennies when the boy and his parents come out of the dining room. I see them dither in the foyer a while, deciding what to do, then they leave and cross the car park into the village.

'Pontoon,' Mary says.

'*Again?*'

She sets her cards down on the table.

'Ah well, I'm done in anyhow. Think I'll go up to bed.'

A fist of wind thumps the glass. Must be what woke me. Yes, there it is again. Takes a minute for my eyes to adjust then I locate the window, only it's in the wrong place. I turn over in bed; jerk my head back. A woman, no idea who she is. Bloody hell. There'll be ructions, I'll have to – no, hang on, wait a minute. It's Mary.

Best not wake her. I look for my hand-clock, see it on the bedside table beside me. My eye things are there too, so I needn't clatter about, just get some clothes on and then I'll be on my way. Be at Sandham Cove before sunrise.

I creep downstairs and out into the car park. Lamps are still burning. Cold morning for it. I check my wrist, but the hand-clock's not there, didn't pick it up. No matter. One of the other lads'll have a clock. Barry Pigeon. I'll have a look in on him when I get there. He'll have marked out his spot already.

Tommy.

Mary's voice. I look around for her, but she's not here. That'll just be her in my head then. I hear her sometimes, putting me right.

His name's Tommy Pigeon.

Can't be, I tell her, what sort of a name's that? She'll be right, though, no doubt.

'Come on, Tommy,' I say. 'I'll carry your eye things, you take the sack.'

No answer. He must've gone on ahead. Keen as muck he is. That's right, I remember now, told him I'd say bye to Mary then catch him up. I expect she's gone to pick the kids up. Got to get going anyway, don't want to miss it. I look at the sky, the shell of the moon, no bombers though. By God, that wind, nearly blows you off your feet.

I cross the road, see the castle ahead. Should've put my big coat on 'cos there's snow now too, just a few flakes, trying their luck. I go through a gate, get into the shelter of a hedge. Almost forgot the way for a second, but no, this is right, I remember now. Sometimes I forget things, Mary'll tell you. That's it, here's the bridge with the stream that's always gargling under it. Tough going in this wind, mind. I have to lean into it, put me head down to meet each blast. Not far now. Tommy'll have a brew on in his tent I expect, warm us up. Yes, you see that fence post with the large stone beside it? There, just on the other side of that it's the dunes.

The path's thinning.

SINGLE FILE, MEN, HEADS DOWN!

The wind's blowing straight off the sea, breaks my stride a couple of times then a big gust punches me and I fall against the wall.

HOLD THE LINE THERE! *HOLD* THE LINE!

Heck, what a night. I find my feet again, straighten up, march on. My ear's stinging, but I pay it no mind and before long I reach the path that squirrels into the dunes. A bush snags me as I pass, tearing a hole in my fleece.

I told you to take your big coat, soaked through, you daft ha'peth.

'Ah, Mary, there you are. It's tonight. I'm finally going to see it.'

See what, love?

I look up at the sky. 'Planes, three, no, five! It's all right, they're ours.'

They're past me in a flash. Climb a dune, get a proper look from there, but the grass is a real pain, keeps getting wound round me feet. One more dune then it's the beach.

Careful. You fall at your age, you break something.

I'm all right, don't be fussing. By Hell, it's all up and down though, takes the puff out of me. Tommy'll be laughing his head off. Does a mile in under five minutes, Tommy, makes dust of the lot of us. Aye well, I'm coming, you bugger. I half-run, half-slide to the bottom of the dune and then look around.

You should come back now, love, get warm.

All right, *all right.* Chattering on, can't a man think? Which way? There's the path now, something lying on it. Looks like a rock, but it's not a rock. It's a bird, shot down. Your mates have left you, I tell him, no choice, that's how it is sometimes.

'Tommy!'

He'll have some tea, Tommy will, p'raps even something a bit stronger to keep the cold out. My teeth are clattering. Just along this way, got to be. All I have to do is stay inside the moment then I can keep it whole.

This way, you silly sod. You're losing yourself again, look.

She's right. Coming, love. Always knows what to do, Mary.

I hear the sea before I see it; angry as hell, but then I cross the beach and it's like it lights up the whole sky, nothing in front of me except waves, white, all white, rising, falling, hurling themselves against the cliffs. The spray stings my eyes.

Can't see Tommy. No one else from my unit either, but I'm sure they said here. Got me wires crossed probably. I see a tooth of rock jutting out of the sand: a monster, might be the head of a dragon, or just a dressing gown on the back of the door. Not real.

Go back to sleep, love. Just a dream.

Something's trickling down my neck. My hand finds a cut on my ear, wet with blood, but I don't remember how it got like that. The wind comes at me again, another whack, but I know I'm no match for it, so I just sit down on the sand.

That's right, love, get your breath back.

I've forgotten where she is. Mary, my Mary. Not here. Well, thank God she's not, it's not safe. I'll just lay low 'til Tommy comes. I think I can hear him, his voice calling, but I can't work out what he's saying. Too far away. Several voices now, there must be somebody with him.

I crane my neck. Radio calls, are they? Yes, that's it. Just the one plane at first, then I see others dropping down through a thick stretch of cloud. Dark shapes, a whole row of Vs, at least three squadrons. Another group to my right, even bigger, too many to count. Our boys, look, it's our boys coming home.

I stagger to my feet, snatching at my eye things, but they're twisted, can't get them up to my face in time. Where you at, man, you're missing it. No greater sight than a Spitfire squadron, Tommy. That'll put the fear of God into 'em. Listen to that roar.

Another gust, I'm not braced, it drops me to my knees. I haul myself up just in time to see two fall from the sky, spiraling, like they're made of nothing, scraps of paper. They crash on the beach a hundred yards ahead, but before I can reach them another comes straight at me, losing height. It swerves to my right, heads out to sea and then hits the water with a smack.

There's hundreds, Tommy, almost fill the sky, but they shouldn't be trying to land in this storm. They don't stand a chance.

I stagger forward, trying to reach the wreckage of one that's just come down, only it isn't there anymore. I turn, scan the beach, gone, just a feathery thing there now, a what's-it, a bird, aye, that's it, lying on his back, poor thing. I reach out to right it, but it struggles, beats its wings, then he slips sidewards, all the fight gone from him. Another there. This one's hit the deck so hard his head's come clean away. They're everywhere now, dead or dying.

A churring of wings makes me look up again. It's the biggest group yet, but no sooner have they dipped below the clouds than the rank breaks. Some ditch into the dunes, others find shelter in a crevice on the cliff, safe, but only for a minute. I watch as the waves pick them off and one after the other, they fall into the sea. So many. I wander among them, gazing at their broken bodies, wings torn, necks twisted, eyes glazed and staring at the starless sky.

A light further along the beach, swinging left and right, an odd dance, then I see him, just his outline at first. Tommy, at last. He's running toward me.

'You're bleeding,' he says, skidding to a halt.

'There you are.'

He's taking off his coat. He wraps it around my shoulders. I feel its warmth.

'Everybody's out looking for you.'

'I got separated.'

I point to the bodies lying around us, but he's not got the stomach for it, he's busying himself with the coat, trying to do up the whizzer, but his fingers are too cold.

'The others all went to the causeway,' he says. 'They thought you'd try to get across to the mainland. But then I remembered what you said in the hide.'

No wonder then. There's been a right cock up. They're not supposed to be at the causeway, they're meant to be here. He's scrabbling inside the pocket of the coat, gets this thing out, what it's called? Lights up. He's jabbing at the thing. Phone. That's it.

Daft beggar, he's not Tommy. He's the Moorhen chick. Tommy was here a minute ago though, wasn't he? Where's he gone? I look for him, but there's just the boy.

Sandham Cove he keeps saying.

'They're coming. Think you can make it into the dunes? It'll be more sheltered there.'

I nod. Likes taking pictures. Thinks I'm glass. Nice lad. I reach for his hand, but he takes my wrist instead, a roman handshake. We have to step around the birds. The white belly of the plover, the red throat of the swallow, the black neckerchief of the little ringed plover.

'Lot's made it,' he says.

I look at him.

'No, really, I saw them. Bound to lose a few, right?'

'Aye.'

'C'mon, Mary'll be worried.'

Mary. I picture her now. She's in her blue dress, looking at me across a table.

'You don't want to worry her.'

No, I don't want to worry her. Back home to Mary. I'll tell her about Tommy and the crash landings and how I got separated. She'll know what to do •

Sea Glass

THE HOUSE is restless. I hear it in the walls, a skin-on-skin sound, then gargles and clacks like it's clearing its throat. I take a book – one of the set texts on Shakespeare's sonnets - to the window seat in the bedroom, padding the small space with cushions as a child would, and climb into it. I can't focus on the words. I already know I'm not going back in the Autumn, yet now and then I play the role of student, Mum's voice needling. Coming away was meant to help put things in perspective, but what are those things? I don't know. I picture Mum with the women from her bridge club, drinking tea from a painted cup, telling them how brilliantly Tom's doing at medical school, and then, without pausing for breath, how her high-achieving daughter is taking a 'study break' by the sea.

I stare out of the window; the storm's closer now, spreading like ink. I rub away the mist of my breath and try to guess the direction the dark clouds are headed. *Am* I doing better here? It's hard to tell. Some days

I don't get up at all, just lie rolled up in the duvet. Other days, I force myself to walk, going up behind the house onto the moorland path, steeling myself to keep going until the light fades. Once, I caught the smell of a fox, but I didn't see him. Later, he found me, a backward glance as he trotted off. As for people, I don't see them much, though I hear them sometimes on the beach, laughter, a dog yapping. I could go into the village, into one of the pubs where men drink at the bar, but the thought makes me sick with anxiety. And yet I was someone who did that once, went alone to a pub on the off chance I'd meet friends.

Sometimes I'd settle for strangers.

You don't look yourself, Em.

Jane... on the last day of term. She was worried; searching for something to explain the skipped lectures, the missed parties, the long hours spent alone. She looked at me intently as if the answer might be written on my face, but she couldn't read it. Later, in bed, the thick felt of darkness around me, I pressed my fingers to my face, probing cheekbones, nose and jaw. I didn't *feel* any different.

It's dark when the storm finally comes. I count the seconds between thunder and lightning and, in the flashes, see the white cuff of waves at the base of Brimham Rock. Rods of rain beat the windows. I move to the stairs, sit halfway up and look at the ceiling, feeling the dust from the cracks settle on my upturned face. The light bulb sways back and forth, seconds of darkness then a skin-tingling buzz of electricity as it flickers on again. Then, another gust; it bears down on the roof, presses in. I feel it in my teeth, the house beginning to unbuckle itself from the rock.

I'm not sure when the storm passed, but when I wake I'm on the window seat again, a blanket wrapped tightly around my shoulders. I listen for the house, but it's silent, startled mute. There are new wounds though, plaster chips in the hallway and the letterbox hangs from a single screw.

The sun's peering over the horizon. I go out through the back door to gulp the electric coolness with big, open-mouthed breaths. A fishing boat is heading out, rocking side to side as it breaks over the waves. The gulls are following it. I could go to the beach to rake over the sea's gifts, but my legs are heavy. I'm tired, more tired than I should be so I go back in, climb the stairs and, halfway, unable to bear the effort of keeping it around my shoulders, I let the blanket fall.

You're such an odd shape.

A memory of Mum bringing out dresses for me to try on. What would I be? Nine or ten. Martha's there, my Aunt, clouding the air with cigarette smoke.

Stand straight, Emma.

Stepping nakedly into first one dress, then the next, while she turns me at the hips.

It's her shoulders, they stick out, look, the way it hangs on her... if only she was longer in the body...

I push the memory away and crawl into bed. There's a strangeness gathering in the house, even in the inanimate things: the chair, the curtains, the clothes that lie crumpled on the floor. They've a kind of knowingness about them that makes me feel excluded. Even the finds I've arranged on the windowsill – the long line of sea glass, the arm of driftwood - seem to belong to someone else. I pull the duvet over my head, drifting into a heavy, dreamless sleep.

When I wake again, hours later, it's to a sound I can't place. I think it might be my mobile – Mum, Dad, Jane – but it doesn't feel like it was ringing. I try to summon it again, this sound that plays at the edge of my senses, but I can only make out the soft *kscch* of the waves. Then I hear it again, it reaches me on a breath from the window. A murmuring, almost a voice. I get up and look out, but it's dusk and the gulls are coming in, a raft of white on white. They are an unruly, raucous gang and as they get closer their cries drown everything out. It's only when I'm outside on the rocks, looking down into the foamy cud, straining every part of me to reach for the sound that I hear it again, as clearly as if the sea had pulled me close and whispered in my ear. It's an urgent hiss, not unpleasant, no words I can make out, yet it feels meant for me.

I glance back at the house, see the jealous glint of its windows then I clamber down the rocky path onto the beach. The tide line is higher up and bigger than it was before the storm: a coil of blue, frayed rope, razor shells netted in sand-rimed kelp. I lift clumps of it with both hands, shaking out cockles, crab claws, bottle tops, searching for the gleam of glass. I haven't wanted to stray too far since coming to the house, but today I go further than I've been before, to where the bay narrows to a crescent point and the upturned boats lie in rows on the sand.

There, at last, I'm rewarded – a piece of sea glass, sapphire blue, polished marble-smooth. I carry it for a while, this new treasure;

rolling it around in my palm or holding it in my pocket. Every time I let go of it, I feel a tweak of loss until my fingers find it again. I'm tempted to take it back to the house to let it find its place in the long line on the bedroom windowsill, but underneath all the other sounds the sea is talking again. I stand for a long time, listening. If I close my eyes, I can feel the sound of it in my throat. Slowly, I strip off my clothes and walk into the water until I'm neck deep, wait for the next wave. It lifts me, like I'm being carried to bed, and as I float out, the sea begins to move over me. It is slow and steady work, whittling me down, smoothing the angles of my body, blunting the edges of my elbows and shoulder blades.

The following morning, skin still taut with salt, I felt a peace I'd not felt for months. The sea's work had made me happy. I swim now whenever I can summon the energy and each time stay in the water until my body is stiff with cold. The house never wants me to go, of course. When I put my ear to the wall, I hear it asking me to stay, but then I look at my new shape, at the sea's fine work, and it pleases me.

He'd been ringing for days, he said. He stands in the kitchen doorway looking at me with tears in his eyes. I remember exactly when I last saw him cry. It was my tenth birthday and we were watching E.T at the cinema. He wanted to go home because he was dying - E.T, not Dad.

'Where is she?' I say, pulling a blanket up around my shoulders.

'You know, Mum. She's...' The words die on his lips. 'She'll come, she just thought it'd be better if it was me this time.'

She's still angry with me for dropping out. She's probably found out I sold the Beetle too. No need for a car if I'm not going back. His eyes rest on my wrists. It burns him to look at me, so he lets his eyes wander, takes in the plaster dust that's settled on everything. He never used to comment on how I looked anyway so I don't mind he doesn't say anything now. Mum's always taken care of that.

'How are you doing?

'Fine.' A silence settles around what I can't say, and he can't ask.

He moves hesitantly to one of the kitchen chairs, but he doesn't sit down. 'It's further out of town than I thought it'd be.'

'Is she still angry?'

'She's... worried. She wants you to come home so she can look after you.'

'So she can work on me full time, more like. No, thanks.'

'She cares about you, Emma.'

'So where is she?'

He stares at his shoes. They have a crud of wet sand along the edges, but the tops are polished the way she likes them.

'Why do you put up with her, Dad?'

He opens his mouth to make a well-rehearsed protest.

'No, really, why do you? She bullies you, she bullies all of us. Why do you think Tom chose New Zealand to go to medical school? New Zealand, for God's sake?'

'Is that what this is about? A spat with your mother?'

'You're changing the subject.'

'I don't feel bullied.' He sees me roll my eyes. 'Yes, she can be a little...forceful, she's been a bloody nightmare since you told her you're not going back. But it's because she cares.'

'She's told you to bring me home, hasn't she? That's what you're really doing here.'

'She thinks...we both think...' He takes a step toward me, but a plaster chip falls from the ceiling, narrowly missing his head and landing on his shoulder. He stares at it, looks up. I hadn't noticed it before, but the ceiling has opened up a little where two cracks meet. You can see the grey of plaster, the edge of what might be a beam.

'Has anyone looked at that?'

'What are you doing here, Dad? If it really is to take me home – '

'It wasn't, but now I've seen you...' He turns away, grips the kitchen counter with both hands. 'You don't have to be on your own with this, Emma. Me and Mum, we can get you help. Maybe you could even take a sabbatical from university, or whatever they call it. We could talk to them, bound to have a department for this sort of thing.'

He's not sure what 'this sort of thing' is. I close my eyes, and summon again the feeling of the sea mouthing my skin.

Before he leaves, we stand together on the edge of the rocks and there, just for a moment, I think I could tell him everything, make him understand. We could have secrets like we used to have, sneaking off to the cinema when I was supposed to be doing my homework, taking the back road to my piano lesson which always made me late, but meant he could drive fast over the bumps.

Just come home. His voice or the waves, I don't know which.

That night, I walk into the sea again; wading out until the water closes around my throat; then the waves lift me, and I float out into the bay until the lights of the village are a blur. I can smell the kelp on the beach letting go of the day's heat. I am alive. I am the sea's embrace. I am weightless.

I'm sleeping when, days later, they return. The sound of the engine on the drive jerks me awake. Mum's with him this time, but it isn't until I get downstairs I realise there are others too, a man and a woman. They let themselves in to the kitchen, all talking at once; then Mum sees me, and screams.

The woman snatches up a throw from the sofa to cover me.

'Christ, Emma,' Mum says, fighting for a breath. 'What the hell have you done to yourself?'

She hasn't seen me naked for years, but it's not that. She looks like she's got something in her mouth she needs to spit out. She never did like my shape; clearly she doesn't think much of the new one either.

'What's going on?' I ask.

They exchange glances, but nobody answers. Dad starts opening cupboards looking for mugs. The man is first to sit down. I don't like the look of him. He has a bag he nudges under the table with his foot. Maybe it's got a taser in it, or one of those strait jackets.

The woman starts talking, steers me to a chair. 'I'm Mandy,' she says. 'And this is Andrew. We're from the Meadows. It's a treatment centre for eating disorders. I know that must sound a bit scary, but we're just here to have a chat.'

'Like hell you are.'

'Sit down,' Mum snaps.

It's raining outside now; it darkens the room. The walls are whispering, the stone flags getting hot, burning the soles of my feet. *It's all right*, I say, silently, *they'll go soon.*

Mum does most of the talking, a one-sided conversation. She walks as she talks, her heels clacking on the floor; she opens cupboards, looks in the fridge, trips over her words when she finds them empty. 'It's obvious to everyone this thing's got out of hand.' Her voice comes from the crevices of her mouth. It sounds calm, rehearsed, but it's edging up. 'It's time for you to listen to other people, people who know – '

'I'm not leaving the house.'

'This?' A fleck of spit shoots from her mouth. 'You sold the car to rent this shithole? Do you know how many hours your father worked on that car?'

'When did you last eat something?' Andrew says. His eyes are cold.

35

He waits for my answer, but Mum interrupts.

'Is it a boy?' she says. 'All this, because of a boy? Someone at uni?'

I open my mouth to say something, but the house gets there first, flushing a breath of soot and gull shit down the chimney.

'No one's forcing you do anything,' Mandy says. Her hand touches my arm, but I pull back. 'We're here to help you.'

She exchanges a look with Andrew. He's tense, coiled.

'Tea?' Dad says. 'I think we were all going to have some tea, weren't we?'

'It isn't a *boy.*'

I think of telling her about Lenny from the Dickens. He'd been the last, hadn't he? Got me down as one of those nice Home Counties girls who didn't give it out easy. He'd talked about Thomas Hardy and Brexit, made his pint last all night, fucked me with his socks on.

'Then what is it?'

Andrew and Mandy look at each other. This isn't what they were expecting. They thought they'd be in charge.

'Well, whatever it is this isn't the right place for you. You need to get some clothes on, get a shower too by the looks of you. Look at your hair, it's like straw.'

I finger strands of it, sand and salt powdering the table.

'Nothing's ever as bad as it looks, Emma. You've got five weeks before term starts again...*leave the tea, George, for Heaven's sake!*'

Dad sets down two mugs on the table, and then, dithering, turns back for the other two. Andrew gets up to help. I see my chance. I leap out of my chair and hurl myself at the back door. It opens with a smack. Andrew flings a hand out to grab me, knocking over a mug. A cry of anguish, the house, or Dad. For a second I'm blinded by the rain, then I see the waves breaking over the rocks. Andrew's behind me, his shoes skidding on the path. It's further than I remember, and I trip on a stone, sliding several feet on my back. I scramble up; hear Mum's voice yelling from the top, then I'm there, teetering on the edge. A wave, foaming all along its crest, I reach out to meet it.

I'm swimming then, dropping my head under for as long as my breath allows, clawing the waves when I surface. When I look to the shore I see Andrew heeling off his shoes; he dives in, but the sea pushes him back, huge waves that slop into his mouth. I kick away, let myself be pulled out to where the water is deep and cold. And then, when I am far enough out, the sea starts to work on me again, more urgently now.

It rolls me, turns me, whittles me down. *You don't need them,* it says, *you don't need air.* I shed the last buttery fat of my breasts; feel the angles of my shoulders and hips smoothed away.

I lose the last of me.

Sometime, years from now perhaps, a girl with straw-coloured hair will walk along the beach, alert for anything that catches the light, and pulling back a frond of kelp, happen upon my new shape, as smooth and polished as sea glass and find it beautiful •

Lake House

IT WAS to be our last summer at the house though of course we didn't know it then. Closing my eyes, I still recall that heat-tired afternoon: Dad lighting the barbeque ready for the guests arriving, Beth on the porch raking through her bucket, her tangled hair smelling of lake rot, and Mum, upstairs, getting ready for the party.

I sat on her bed while she did her make-up and watched. Freshly bathed, she spread out brushes of different sizes on the dresser, pots of cream, powder cases with lids that clicked shut. She spoke of things I didn't understand. Perhaps she wasn't really talking to me, more to herself, but then she met my reflected eyes in the mirror and told me a strange fact: how a man liked to kiss a woman's throat because it was where a predator held its prey to suffocate it.

'Like a fox? Or a weasel?'

'Yes,' she said, and smoothed cream over the hollow in her neck, brushing her hands in sharp upward strokes until her skin glowed.

Eyelids: mallard green; cheeks: dog-rose pink. She put her scent on last, placing two fingers on an upturned bottle, dabbing behind her ears. Then, eyes shining, she snaked a trail over her jugular and my nostrils filled with that hot, musky smell so reminiscent of their bedroom on Sunday mornings.

'Off you go now,' she said. 'Play.'

And so I left her, feeling peculiar, fat as a seedpod, ready to burst – I had to run, run fast, to the lake, or along the beach. It didn't matter where. Seeing me zip through the gate at the far end of the garden, Beth sprang up from the porch and ran after me.

She caught up as I joined the path to our beach. We had a secret beach, Beth and me, inaccessible to all but the most determined. The path was one we'd made ourselves. We clambered over branches that leaned into the water, their gnarled roots wet and dark. The earth there was sandy clay and sucked at our feet, but we kept on, carving a way through brambles and then picking our way through thick stalks of willowherb.

'Someone's been here,' Beth said. 'Look, they've gobbed.' She was pointing at a willowherb leaf.

'It's cuckoo spit.'

'A cuckoo is a bird and birds don't spit.'

'A froghopper bug makes it. There's an egg inside.'

'Where?' She peered at the froth. 'Show me it then.'

Eager to be right, I scooped the foam onto my hand and spread it thinly across my palm to reveal not an egg, but a single golden froghopper, not yet adult. Beth gazed at it, unimpressed, and then, shocking dozens of damselflies from the flower heads, she darted off.

I looked at the nymph, deprived of its nest and tried to undo what I'd done, to cover it up again, but the froth dissolved on my skin and the nymph dropped off my hand.

Beth, yelling. She'd got to the secret beach. We often rested there, stretched out for hours on the sliver of sand. I didn't think anyone one else knew about it, though I reckoned it was possible to swim up to it from the next bay. I'd never tried. I couldn't swim and it didn't bother me, not really, but Dad hated it.

Don't know what we're paying that bloody woman for. Isn't right a boy your age not knowing how to swim. I'll teach you.

I'd been having swimming lessons with Mrs Dunleavy for almost a year, in a group first, then one-to-one. Her voice sounded like a thousand voices in that echoey space.

'Paddles!' And she'd make a shape with her hands, pushing imaginary water back. 'You can't sink, you're a cork, you'll bob right back up.'

But it didn't matter what she said or how hard I tried. My body resisted the water.

I'll teach you.

I don't remember exactly when he said it, perhaps on one of the afternoons we'd gone out in the boat, me tugging at the life jacket that scratched my chin. I only know my stomach chewed on his words for days. I knew he hadn't meant in a pool. He'd meant the lake, but to me the lake was full of terrors. Those I saw who swam in it were not afraid of the depths, whereas I imagined a million hungry mouths beneath the surface.

Beth again, tugging at my t-shirt. 'Look!'

She was walking at the water's edge looking for treasures: stones, bits of chipped pottery she found mixed in the gravel. Every now and then she swooped on something interesting and washed it off in the shallows. I still see her so vividly. In my mind, it's always that summer and she's always seven. Skinny and small, bony hips and shoulder blades that jutted out her back like oars. Later, as we walked home that night, Beth slightly ahead, I remember how I'd likened my steady footfall to an adult's. I was only older than her by five years, but I felt the weight of it - the responsibility, a nag that followed me around, a knowledge that for all she had the strength of a gale the world was too big for her. I had to keep her safe.

A mash of voices and music reached us as we opened the gate and then we were amongst the grown-ups. I took in all that'd changed since we left: fatty cruds of meat chewed to the bone, buckets of ice, tiny columns of ash that shuffled across the table in the breeze. Those people are faceless, now, many of them, but I remember the pressure of their eyes on me. And then Mum, floating in her long dress, glided over to where we stood, her cigarette filter stained red.

'My wanderers! My beautiful children.'

She jangled and clinked with the jewelry she only wore for parties - and she cradled us, one arm stretched to cover us both, the other reaching for her drink.

How dazzling she was. Tanned from the long days in the sun, lips like sugar melting. We fetched trays of cheese and fruit to offer around and when there wasn't any more, we sat on the porch and watched while the adults played charades, drank cocktails, their cigarettes pricking the dark. Sometimes they goaded each other to dance, but it was only Mum who did. She made circles on the lawn, the strap of her dress falling off her shoulder, her arms turning first this way then that like reeds under water. Every so often she'd remember us, reclaim us, and plant a hot sticky kiss on the back of my neck, but then someone would speak to her and she'd lean into them and her hand would drop away.

Dad was there too, of course, sitting in a deck chair, watching her. Always watching her. Once, Beth went to stand beside him while he pulled at his drink in great glugs. He fished out an ice cube for her to suck on and when she returned to the porch to sit beside me, I could hear it, the cube clacking off her teeth and then the crunch as she shattered it to bits.

The party went on long after we'd gone to bed, late into the night, I watched from the window seat in our room - the light of a dozen citronella candles flickering across flushed faces - then got back into bed beside Beth and listened. Voices, the odd sentence - it wasn't possible to hear much above the music - but then the record player was switched off and the only people I heard were Mum and Dad.

Mum's voice, no longer a melody: 'Oh, for God's sake, not *that* again!' Dad's voice rumbling on, nothing I could make out. Hers again.

'Andrew...? So what if he did...? It didn't *mean* anything.'

My mind filled in the blanks and as I lay listening a bubble of suspicion rose from some unknown depth and formed an image, it might've been a memory or something I'd made up: a man, rising and falling into the cradle of a woman who could so easily have been our mother.

Their raised voices swirled and slapped against our bedroom window long into the night. Beth, who had fallen asleep, let out a little moan. Were the monsters in her dreams worse than our parents?

It could've been a day or a week between Dad's first mention of teaching me to swim and us going together to the lake. Fear has a way of stretching time. I only know it was early morning and it threatened rain. To begin with, there were just thick columns in the distance over the hills, but I could smell it coming closer. The air was slack, metallic-tasting and then suddenly the storm was all around us; a torrent. It needled my head and drummed on the back of my neck, funneling down between my shoulder blades. My arms roughened with hundreds of tiny bumps. It didn't deter him though. We were doing it, he said. And so, on the beach, Dad stripped down to his trunks and waded in, then he turned to wait for me. Reluctantly, I followed, bits of stone and gravel lodged between my toes. As first his thighs and then his trunks got wet, I found myself staring at his groin, the thin material clinging to the sleeping curve that rested there.

He began by demonstrating front crawl, splashing, twisting and flexing, muscle and sinew and bone all perfectly aligned, then he stopped, trod water, and shook droplets from his head.

Now you try.

I hesitated, thinking of Mum back at the house, curtains drawn, sheathed in darkness, her secret scent filling the bedroom. I'd have done anything to be there, to dive into that warm fug as I used to do before Beth was born, when I'd plant my cold feet on Mum's shins and fold myself into her soft body.

I waded in, splashed a few strokes.

No, no. Get your head in the water.

Rain pattered around us, the lake an oily canvas that held each drop suspended on the surface for the briefest of seconds before it dissolved. I tried again, scooting forward, but the water swallowed me, and I sank. He hauled me back up.

For Christ's sake! Not like that.

That was the end of the lesson, though he didn't say as much, just turned away and waded to the shore in a steady veil of rain.

As the summer wore on, I began to walk further and further from the house to where the river slid into the lake, away from my parents. In that tunnel of growth, I could imagine I was in a different world, lifting rocks in search of caddis fly, trying to spot which bit of twig might encase a nymph. Even the sun struggled to reach me, only now and then blinking through a canopy of trees, dappling the water, reminding me to look up: a barbed wire fence at the top of the slope, a field beyond it, a pile of rocks that might once have been a cattle shed or even a house.

I no longer told Beth where I was going, though somehow, she always found me. I couldn't talk to her. I felt restless, irritable, as though my skin was too tight. I was changing and yet I didn't know how. As I got closer to the lake, the currents thickened to rapids, breaking over rocks in bubbly tendrils of foam. Here, the water was charged with a kind of knowing, carrying messages to the lake from other rivers and hills. Suppose I didn't go back? I wouldn't have to swim again with Dad. I'd simply emerge from the mouth of the river, but instead of being dragged under the lake I'd float high above it, circling the water before flying over our garden. And I'd see them, our parents, two scorched bodies on sun loungers. And I'd hear the thread of music coming from the record player inside the house and their voices, scratching away at each other.

A dream. Back in the real world, I turned to look at Beth who was a few feet to my right. She'd taken the hardest route across the stones, her bare feet curled over a rock. She pulled a rope of river-soaked hair from her mouth - the same dark blonde as Mum, but in every other respect she was more like Dad: the way she narrowed her eyes at a task, how they darkened from burnished blue to black whenever she was in a temper, even her walk had something of his confidence. They irritated me, those similarities, though I'd never noticed them before. I watched her feet disappear into the rapids, imagined them being sucked into invisible crevices where she might get trapped, where she might snap. Maybe I wanted her to. But then she jumped out onto the bank to safety, strong and sinewy as an ash sapling.

Why did I measure myself against her and not the older boys I saw by the lake, who came with their kayaks, scraping them along the beach, who gobbed into face masks to stop them steaming up and wrestled flippers onto sandy feet? Who weren't afraid.

I'd hoped that first disastrous swimming lesson might be the last, that Dad would see it didn't matter what he did or said, I couldn't improve, but no, each morning he woke me early and we went to the lake. Always, the water was the same silvery grey, perfectly smooth, and as we waded in the heat of our bodies rubbed a hole in the mist. A moment of peace, and then:

Head over to the side, ear in the water. IN the water. Right, now bring your arm over and turn, breathe. BREATHE.

I kept trying to stand up. I didn't like the feeling of so much dark beneath me.

Stop putting your feet down. STOP putting your feet down.

We inched forward, me cartwheeling my arms over my head. I swallowed more water, coughed, tried to stop my teeth chattering.

You've got to put your head in.

The lake looked on, still, knowing my fear. I pictured Beth in the house, waking to find me gone and scrabbling into the space beside Mum in bed, curling into the arc of her body.

We've got to sort these legs out!

My wrists were red from where he held them. He got me to lie flat on my stomach, his right hand pushed up against my belly button, then he pulled it away and took hold of my ankles.

Kick! Up, down, up, down.

But I was a fish on a hook. I tried to wrench my feet away, clawing the water with my hands, twisting until I got one foot free. It hit something. My toes stinging, I turned, saw Dad clutching one side of his face.

He was breathing hard, furious, then he let out a roar and waded past me to the shore. I didn't follow. I stood in the water for a time and then sat alone on the beach, cold, and gazed out over the lake. Its surface had sealed again like we'd never entered it.

In the days that followed the bruise on Dad's cheek blossomed: black, purple, several shades of green, but he never mentioned it and, miraculously, with each lesson I began to notice improvements. I was able to match the movement of my arms to my breaths, first with my feet on the lakebed and then alone in short bursts. Before long I could swim ten meters, then fifty, and soon I could leave him behind, swim out far into the lake until his voice was small.

I began to seek out bigger challenges then, once even swimming all the way to the river, daring myself to go on even as the shore slipped into shadows. I relished my new freedom, staying out late until there was only darkness above and below and a thin moon. There, with only the quiet breathing of the lake, I found I could forget everything – Mum weaving her silken thread around the men in the garden, creating nests of secrets. Dad watching.

How easy it is now to flush out memories and then deliberately overlay them with different ones – happier...late afternoon, Dad in a crisp, clean shirt, giddy, he and Mum talking about my swimming, Mum calling me her 'big man'. Dad lifting me up in his arms and spinning me around.

'Faster than a dolphin, aren't you, Matty? Show her how you do your breaststroke.'

And I'd transform myself into a frog on the lawn while they looked on. I blew air into imaginary water, straining to lift my head up while Mum told us how Dad had always been a good teacher. He'd taught her to fish, years ago. For a while then, listening to her reminisce about their youth, hearing him laugh, I could imagine we were a different family, one that knew how to be together.

Only Beth ruined it. She became increasingly whiney, grumpy when I tried to get her to play some game or other; easy to goad. It wasn't fair, she said, she wasn't allowed to show anyone how well *she* could swim.

'Because you can't,' I said.

'You could teach her,' Dad said, smiling. 'Tomorrow.'

'Me?'

It felt like a prize. The perfect solution. And nothing, not even Beth's disappointment at getting me instead of Dad, could spoil it.

The sky was polished blue as we set off for the beach the next morning, me and Dad carrying chairs and towels, Beth and Mum a bucket of ice and a cooler bag full of food. We cleared a patch of sand, chucking sticks into the bushes, and then Mum went for a swim, her chin balanced on the water, cheeks puffed out like sails. When she got out Dad handed her a wrap, playfully snatching it away from her so she had to dive for it. Then she was reaching for a cigarette and asking him to uncork the wine.

I couldn't wait to get in the water. I wanted to show Dad how fast I was, but Beth was already nagging him to take her in.

'You take her,' he said. 'Have a swim yourself though first. Go on, I'll watch.'

I bounded through the shallows until I was on tiptoes then dipped my head under to wet my hair before swiveling around to see if he was looking. He waved. Then I was off, swimming front crawl as fast as I could, the crush of water around my ears. I swam all the way to the beach where the lake met the edges of a farm and then stopped, panting, looking back again, but I'd gone much further than I thought and Mum, Dad, and Beth were small. I found my feet and made for the shore but pulled up sharply when I noticed it was dotted with sheep shit. Some of it had even got in the water, dissolving into thick green clouds near to where I stood. I spat several times, sick at the thought that the water I'd been swimming in had touched the shit. The sheep in the field, startled from their grazing, eyed me warily then scattered in all directions, their tails trembling like catkins.

45

I was sure when I returned, I'd be told off for having kept Beth waiting, but nobody seemed to notice I was back until I was among them, dripping wet. Beth was showing Mum things from her bucket, Mum with her head tilted to the side of her chair, half-looking, half-peering at the screen on her phone. Dad picked up her empty glass from the sand at her feet and poured her another drink.

'Did you see me, Dad?' I said. 'I swam all the way to that beach over there.'

'Hmm....?'

Beth appeared beside us and began tugging at the hem of Dad's shorts. 'I can swim. I *can.*'

'Go on then. Stay with Matty though.'

She sprinted to the lake, kicking up sprays of water. I chased after her, yelling at her to wait and caught up with her after a few strides. Together, we waded out until she was waist deep.

'You have to stay with me, Dad said. I'm in charge.'

I felt bad tempered though I didn't understand why. It wasn't just one thing, I didn't know what it was: maybe the sheep shit that'd fouled the lake, or Dad who was supposed to have watched me, but hadn't. I glanced back at the beach. He was holding Mum's drink out to her, but she didn't take it. She was looking at her phone. For a moment he just stood there, perfectly still, then he snatched the phone from her hand. She jumped up, the wrap sliding from around her waist.

'Are they watching me?' Beth said.

'No. They're fighting again. There's just us now, get it? You have to do as I say.'

Her eyes darkened. She didn't like this new version of me. She didn't want *me* at all. I knew what she was thinking, that I thought I was better than her because I could swim the way Dad had taught me. He was looking at Mum's phone, spinning away from her as she tried to snatch it.

I grabbed Beth's arm, pulling her back when she tried to swim off. 'Not there, it's too deep!'

She slid away from me, doggy paddle, thrashing about.

'That's *not* how you do it.' I swam in front of her and took hold of her wrists.

'Let me go!'

She broke free and set off again, chin up, puffing out air. After a few strokes she sank. I hauled her up and she emerged struggling, furious, eyes streaming.

'Your face has got to be in the water, or you'll sink.'

'You're a bully!'

'First you have to learn to float – '

'Get out of my way!'

Almost immediately she sank again, her pale skin disappearing into the dark. I dived down and managed to hook my fingers under the strap of her swimsuit. When she broke the surface she slapped the water with both hands and coughed. I glanced behind me to the beach, Mum was jabbing her finger into Dad's face.

'Stop making a fuss, they can see you, you know, being a baby.'

She looked at them too then, for what seemed like several minutes, but was probably only seconds. It's what I remember most clearly, her face in that moment. How much had she been aware of before then? Their bickering, yes, but it was more than that now. I saw it in her eyes, in the sucking in of her bottom lip: fear. Not of being out there on the lake, of being taken under, all the things that'd frightened me; she was seeing our parents as they truly were.

'I don't want you to teach me.'

'This is how it's done. I have to hold you under your tummy and then - '

'I know how to swim!'

My big toe kicked a stone and I yelped. 'No, Beth, you don't!'

The pain made me angrier. I swam further out into the lake, away from her, but she began to doggy paddle after me.

'Go back!'

I kept swimming. Even though I could see she needed me. I could *see* she was tiring. So, then what? *What* was I thinking? A million thoughts, still now I can't make them stop whirring. I remember I put my face under to see if I could see the bottom, but saw only my thighs, yellowish-brown, then nothing. It was still amazing to me that I longer feared it. Seconds only, then, when I came up for air, Beth had gone. I dived under again. Darkness.

My heart lurched. The lake had dragged her down, tricked us both, and now I, too, began to feel its pull. I trod water, but my legs were heavy. Water slopped into my mouth. I could hear Mum's voice, sharp, a boat bumping the water somewhere in the distance.

And then Beth, face down. She floated up to me from the deep.

You can't sink, you're a cork, you'll bob right back up.

I screamed and went on screaming.

Dad heard me first, pushed Mum out the way so hard she fell onto the sand and then he was in the water making great splashes as he leapt through the shallows. I held Beth in my arms, her eyes were open, but she wasn't breathing. She was too heavy and I couldn't turn her, her face kept going under.

'Dad!'

Mum was in the lake now, too, yelling, shouting for help, but there was no one to hear.

Dad reached us. He got Beth off me and then somehow he was swimming on his back, one arm cleaving the water while the other cradled her against his chest. As soon as he got near the beach Mum helped and together, they half-lifted, half-dragged Beth onto the sand. I trailed after them, crying.

Mum was at the table, frantic, scrabbling to find her phone. She knocked the salad bowl flying, swept a wine glass away and then she found her mobile on the sand.

Dad was hitting Beth on her chest with his fist. He'd break her, hammering on her ribcage like that, crush the tiny wet sac that held her heart. I yelled at him to stop and thought of the cuckoo spit and the bug that'd lain hidden and safe in its nest of foam until I destroyed it.

Suddenly, Beth's back arched and, like a blocked drain, she bubbled up water. Quickly, Dad turned her over and she was sick, frothy saliva and lake water erupting from her mouth.

'Beth?' My voice was weak, hardly there at all.

She didn't make a sound, just lay there in Dad's arms, blinking. Mum was clawing at his shoulder, trying to get to her. They carried her back to the house, hurrying, yelling at each other. I didn't go with them. An ambulance arrived: I saw its lights reflected in the windows at the side of the house. I stayed on the beach, shivering, staring at Beth's vomit on the sand.

An hour passed, maybe more. When finally, I went back there was no one home. I wandered from room to room not knowing what to do, then I went and sat on Mum and Dad's bed, the duvet wrapped around my shoulders, while it got dark. I listened for cars on the road, but it was a long time before I heard ours.

Dad. He was by himself. I watched him walk inside and waited, but he didn't come upstairs. I heard him moving around in the kitchen, then a door closed, and it was quiet. I put on my dressing gown and found him sitting in the living room, lights off. Ice settling in a glass next a bottle of whisky.

'Sit down,' he said.

He was holding a cigarette, the ember a fierce dot in the dark. I couldn't see his face, not clearly. I wanted him to shout, needed him to; maybe he'd hit me. I longed for the sting of his hand across my face, but he just sat there, breathing. When he finally spoke again his voice was low, little more than a whisper.

'When I was a boy my Dad took me hunting. He killed a rabbit and made me skin it. I had to hang it from a tree by its legs, make an incision around its backside. Then I pulled back the skin, peeled it off until it hung off its shoulders like a rag.'

'Dad?' He was scaring me. It didn't make sense, his voice, how calm he was. 'Beth - '

'You know the sound cling film makes when you stretch it off the roll?'

'Dad - '

'It was like that. And it smelled dead, you know? No, you don't know.' A stack of ash fell from his cigarette on to the arm of the chair. 'I didn't want to do it. But that's what you do. Eat what you kill or you're not a man.'

She was dead. I knew it. Beth. Beth. The girl who was like him, who was more like him than I'd ever be. I tried to imagine myself in the wood, skinning the rabbit like he'd done, smelling death. All at once sobs burst out of me, too big for my chest. He waited until I stifled them.

'Your sister will be home tomorrow.'

I gulped air, stared at him.

'Now go to bed.'

He left me then. I listened to his feet on the stairs, slow, heavy, the sound of his wedding ring scraping the bannister.

Breathless from crying, I wiped my cheeks on my sleeve and sat in his chair, the leather still warm. He'd put down his glass of whisky on a side table, half-full. I gulped it down, coughed. I wished I'd told him I was afraid of the lake, that even now I felt the pull of the darkness beneath. It would have made a difference. I should've stood up to him.

From the trees at the bottom of the garden came the mournful hoot of an owl; then, minutes later, I heard the soft pattering of rain on the porch. I thought about Beth and the lake water that'd bubbled out of her lungs, and of the dead rabbit, as naked and pink as it'd been at its birth.

I don't know when I fell asleep, only that at some point I moved into the garden and lay on the wet grass. Insects scratching the earth, an animal scuffling in the undergrowth - maybe a fox, maybe a weasel - and underneath it all, as inescapable as the whisper of blood in my ears, the soft lapping sounds of the lake.

There has to be winter

SHE'S HEAVIER than a week ago, rising belly first out of the driver's seat and then walking – no, waddling – round to open the boot to lift out a large carrier bag.

A whiff of chlorine when we embrace. 'How was aqua-natal?'

'Cancelled again. I swam anyway.' She hands me the bag. I peer inside, frozen meals labeled and dated.

'Not *more*, Jane?'

'I was doing a batch. You're only getting what's left over.'

Obviously not true. Ever since the funeral, she'd got into the habit of cooking for me. Initially, I'd encouraged her because it kept her busy and stopped her sitting over me.

'The quiche we can have for lunch,' she says.

I fetch lettuce from the greenhouse and make a salad. I've forgotten to water the pots again, so the leaves are limp. Jane tells me about the 3D scan she's booked.

'You can see the baby yawning, fingernails even. Imagine that.'

I glance at your picture on the mantelpiece, the one I took in Madeira with the sun full on your face. Months ago, I'd placed Jane's first scan photograph beside it and lit a candle. 'How's the pelvic thing?'

'Symphysis pubis dysfunction, it's proper name. I have a belt; do you want to see?'

She angles out from behind the table and lifts her tunic. The naked dome of her belly is a shock. My first thought is to touch it, but I'm afraid if I do, I'll cry. She returns to her plate.

'Does the belt ease it?'

'A little.'

'You're eating well. Not sick anymore that's the main thing.'

'Apparently, everything I eat now just makes more baby fat, but I'm so bloody hungry. Oh, I nearly forgot,' she reaches into her handbag and hands me a leaflet.

'Yoga, Tuesday mornings in the church hall.'

'That'll help your pubic thingy,' I say, dryly.

'For *you*, Mum. You know, perhaps it's time you got out a bit more.'

'Only last week you were complaining you couldn't get me on the phone.'

'Yes, because you don't answer it.'

'Because I'm *out.*'

'Where?'

'Walking.'

'On your own.'

'What's wrong with me walking on my own? Contrary to what you seem to think, I'm not quite ready for a carer.'

'Who said anything about a carer?' She looks at me, wounded. 'I don't see what's wrong with you joining a rambling group.' Silence, then: 'It's been six months.'

'*A whole six months*, is it really?'

'Don't be like that. Just try the yoga, please? If you're not careful you're going to end up as a lonely old lady talking to Dad's photograph.'

She's right, you know, I do talk to your photograph, and not just the one on the mantelpiece, I talk to these, too. They're spread out on the kitchen table now – the last photographs you took after you came out of hospital. You went to the wood as soon as you got off the crutch, every morning without fail. I watched you leave from the window -

your left foot dragging, your shoulders doggedly hunched – and waited anxiously for you to come home, but I never thought of asking you not to go. I couldn't have done that. I look out of the window again now, narrowing my eyes until the garden path blurs. I can see you still, that scruffy old jacket... It's here, you know, hanging on the hook in the understairs cupboard, though its stiffened to a hung shape. I got rid of all of your other clothes, but I couldn't let go of that. I fetch it now and put it on, releasing smells - moss and snow and wind and rain and you – your smell. Thrusting my hands into the pockets, I find a packet of Trebor Extra Strength. Two left in the roll. You got addicted to them when you gave up smoking. Look! Oh, there's a thing, would you look at that. My reflection in the window, see? I've turned into you. I take one of the peppermints from the silver paper and place it on my tongue – communion - and then open the back door.

It's not far to the wood. Across a wooden bridge over a stream, then onto the path you used to take. After fifty yards or so, I plunge into the wood. A white sky where the leaves used to be, trunks of trees, skeletal, statue-grey. My breath curdles the air. Ahead of me a branch tosses; the wind, I think, until I see a squirrel. He stops his acrobatics and twitches his tail like an angry cat. On again; leaves frost-rimed, blackened with rot. Underneath, the ground's slippy, precarious. Instinctively, I grope for something to hold on to and find the branch of a beech tree. It's one of the few trees I can identify; the others are sycamore and oak. You knew them all. You used to explain how you could tell them apart even when they had no leaves. I wish I'd listened more. This tree's roots are thick fingers digging into the earth. I perch on one to rest and look around.

For a long time, it was the birds you came to photograph, but not at the end, your last photos are all of trees. This one, perhaps? Could be. It's hard to identify any individual tree because you liked close-ups: bark, leaves, those warty growths – though you didn't call them that. There was a special word... It won't come, though I know it's on the tip of my tongue. No growths on this tree. I lean in closer and run my hand down its trunk. Smooth, muscular, the way your body felt when you were young. In that flat in Kent, do you remember? We were students. God, it was awful. Damp patches everywhere, fungus on one of the walls. You photographed that too! I close my eyes and rest my cheek against your bark.

'Did you try the yoga?'

'No.'

'Oh, *Mum*.'

'What do you want me to say? Yoga just isn't my thing.' I tidy the 3D scan photos into a neat pile. The baby has rosebud lips just like Jane when she was a baby. I look at her now - irritated, disappointed. Parental.

'Something else then.'

'I'm happy as I am. Stop fussing.'

'You're not happy.'

I bare my teeth in a grin.

'Oh, for Christ's sake! Now you're just being difficult.'

Just for once, I wish she'd stop. She's behaving as if she's the mother and I'm the child, but I can't complain because I've let her do it. I've never actually told her that what makes me happy is going to the wood. And doing yoga in a church hall full of women pretending not to notice one of them's just farted isn't going to help at all.

She touches my arm. 'Mum?'

'What?'

'I'm worried about you.'

'Well, don't be. Actually, I've been thinking I might join the choir.'

'The *choir*?'

I had thought about it, in passing.

'Can you even sing?'

'Well, I used to be able to. Fact, I used to enjoy it.'

No singing in the wood. Too cold even for the birds. I've been walking for over an hour when it starts to snow, just a few flakes at first, then heavier. God, yes, cold, but I don't want to go home and so I find an old stump to sit on and in no time at all a layer of snow clings to me like a second skin. Everything's white. I can almost hear you saying, 'look, look at the light, it's upside down'. And it is, it's coming from the ground now instead of the sky, like the world's turned on its head. There's a faint hiss, too. I can hear it when I hold my breath.

Too cold to sit. Home, put the fire on, have some soup. I know that's what I should do, but I'm too restless there. Your flannel in the bathroom, your watch that still faintly ticks on the dresser. I sit in your chair by the fire, looking out on the view you used to love. But the chair's just a chair. I don't know where you are anymore. Here? Or there?

'You're limping.'

'It's not as bad as it looks.'

'What happened?' She stamps snow off her boots and follows me into the kitchen.

'I slipped on the ice. That bit they never salt on the way into town.'

A plausible lie. I'd actually done it coming back from the wood, caught my foot in a patch of brambles. I wonder why I need to lie at all.

'Have you been to the doctor?'

'With a sprained ankle? No. Did Greg get off to the airport ok?'

'You should have called, Mum. I'd have come and got you. How did you get home?'

'I walked. When's he back?'

'You're sure you're all right?'

'*Yes.*' I take down the mugs from the cupboard, stifle a sigh.

'You could come and stay with us a while.'

'It's a *sprain.*'

'Company, then. It's closer to town. We don't need a reason, do we?'

'Why not go the whole hog and turn the garage into a granny flat?'

'You can be very difficult sometimes, you know.'

'I live *here*. I don't want to leave.'

I can still get to the wood, though I need your stick. I feel your amusement as I hobble along, and sympathy, too. It helps on the rough ground, but not with the brambles. I now have three feet to get tangled up. The wood's changing or I'm changing, seeing things more clearly perhaps. Noticing the detail. All this time I've been frustrated because I've not been able to recognize individual trees, but then suddenly I do recognize one and it's like greeting an old friend.

Your tree. Yes, of course it is. All of your photographs were of this one, I see it now so clearly, all the landmarks you captured with your camera - the wounds. Yes, it's wounded. At some point - not recently – it's suffered a lightning strike down one side. Some branches have been torn off, others withered, dead, though the left side seems to be alive. I have to be near it, to stand where you stood, to see it as you did. I pick a path to it through the fern and then rest my hand against it. My hand, brown age spots, raised veins, wrinkled skin, so much like yours, so much like the bark that it blends in. Other detail, the whorls and the knots, are familiar. There's one of those warty growths and suddenly the word I couldn't remember slips easily into my mind – burr. Burr. I can see why you liked the word. The tree's ancient, perhaps one of the oldest in the wood, but I feel its determination to live, as you must've done, part felled as you were. Next spring these bare, knobbly branches will push out leaves, I'm sure of it. In fact, weren't there leaves in one of your photographs? So, you must've lived long enough to see it in spring. Oh, my love.

I stay with the tree for a few hours, my back against the trunk, looking around the wood, imagining you here. The wood is pinched, turned in, the grey columns of the trees, the blue light thickening between them, the dead bracken, the leafless branches, the puddles rimmed with ice, the black veins of the canopy clotted with empty nests. It all looks like death, but it's not death. There's life here, too, in your wounded tree, under the dead bracken, behind the bark, everything is holding on. Dormant, not dead. Jane's right, there's a time to move on, to pick up the pieces, to get out more, but it shouldn't be instead of this. She wants me to go straight from autumn into spring, and that's just not possible. Not for me, not for anybody. Not for the wood. There has to be a time of darkness, of sap sinking back into the roots.

There has to be winter.

Tunny

HE'S RACING ahead of me now, twisting neatly through a kissing gate, sprinting away again at the other side. It's only when he reaches the steep, rocky path down to the beach he's forced to slow down.

'The sea, Dad!'

A wide stretch, ink-blue and gilded. He pauses for a moment to assess the jump down onto the shingle, then he leaps, leaving a cloud of breath on the air behind him.

Neptune is one of a cluster of small fishing boats moored at the jetty, a fine-looking coble painted white with a blue stripe and a red sail. It used to be Dad's boat, now it's mine; one day, it'll be Billy's. I follow him, my steps heavy on the shell grit, Billy's so light and fast he barely makes a sound. When we get to the boat, he jumps in, climbs down between the benches and turns to take the bait box and rods.

'Going to catch a tunny are we, Billy?'

'Yeah!'

Even after all that running, he's shivering, white with cold, but the hot chocolate will soon warm him up. An extra sweater too, perhaps, once we're out. Hat and gloves? No, Christ, it'll be red-hot come midday. I packed them though, along with a whole lot of other stuff I knew we wouldn't need. I hate it, the planning, the making lists, the endless ticking of boxes, but I daren't give Anna anything to complain about. She already wants these weekends to stop. She says sea fishing's dangerous, what she really means is that I'm not fit to take care of my own child.

As I steer us out along the estuary, I glance back at the town and the hills behind. The banks of whin still cling to night but the sky's already turning a pale yellow. Ahead of us a wreath of herring gulls float on the water.

'After Mason's stack we'll get the sail up,' I tell him, smiling when he opens his mouth to catch the salt spray that kicks over the bow.

As we near the stack, he lifts his binoculars and scoots along the bench. A frothy swell cuffs the base of the rock, but he's looking at the top ledges. He shouts, his words snatched away by the wind, then lowers the binoculars and points. Guillemots.

'You know why the Guillemot lays an oval egg?'

'Yeah, you told me, so they don't roll off.'

I'd forgotten telling him that. Perhaps we'd seen the guillemots on an earlier trip, or we'd read it in the RSPB book of sea birds I gave him for his birthday.

You've got to sort yourself out, Tom.

Anna. Her voice comes to me, a high sung note in my head, but I can't remember when she said it, or where.

Once we're clear of the stack, I raise the sail and the boat surges forward. The light's razor-sharp. Billy leans over the side to dip a hand in the water, snatching it out again when his fingers get too cold. He's happy. Where's the harm? He loves these trips. If only she could see him like this, every weekend he seems a little more mature. What'll he be now? Ten? No, eleven - he starts at secondary school in September. Physically - the roundness of his face, his gappy teeth - he's still very much a child but in every other way he's changing.

We can't go on like this.

I remember now. I'd gone after her. She'd been half-running, stumbling along the beach. I'd grabbed her arm and she'd turned, crying, shouting. It was no use, she had to get away, from our life together, from *me*.

We sail another hour, the sea calm, just small, white tipped waves where the wind grazes the water.

You need to let go.

Let go? We'd had twelve good years. I couldn't just turn and walk away from that. I don't want to think of her, not now, replaying fights long over. I force myself back to the present. 'Want your lunch, Billy?'

'Yeah, I'm starving.'

He looks tired too; the early start catching up with him? Another thing Anna goes on about, she thinks I forget he's just a child. I hand him a sandwich from the rucksack, pour him a cup of hot chocolate and set it down on the bench.

'I'll get your kindle out when you've finished that.'

He bites down on his sandwich, talking over the mouthful. 'I'm all right. I like to watch.'

I always worry he'll get bored. The stories about game fishing I'd read to him at bedtime were exciting. He'd made me read them again and again. The great Lorenzo Mitchell-Henry, tunny fishing's poster boy. We'd looked at the black and white photographs of him and his 851lb fish, the monster tunny that still held the record for the biggest ever caught, but too often the reality was sitting in a boat for hours on end with nothing much happening.

After lunch, I bait up the rods and Billy stretches out on one of the benches to look up at the sky. He starts humming a tune.

'What's that from then?'

'Just something I learned at school.'

He's a natural with the violin. Plays in the school orchestra. Anna never sends me stuff about school, never sends me his reports, just wants me out of his life. Once, I turned up at the school for a concert on the wrong day. Billy's form teacher, Mrs Young, had been nice about it though - must've seen how upset I was - and took me through to the staffroom and made me a cup of tea.

'Gannet!' Billy yells.

It soars in a wide circle behind the boat, ink tipped wings and blonde brow, huge, they're always bigger than you think they'll be. Within minutes, there's a dozen or so, eerily quiet, their eyes fixed on a stretch of water to our right. One breaks rank and drops suddenly, headfirst, folding its wing as it falls, an arrow that speeds past us and pierces the skin of the sea. Moments later, it surfaces with a fish in its beak.

A mackerel. My heart thumps. Where there's mackerel there's tunny. I glance at the rod, but it hasn't moved.

'I'm going to draw them,' Billy says.

'Good idea.'

I go to the rucksack and get out his sketchbook and pencils. We slip again into waiting then, only the sound of Billy's pencil slurring over the paper and the lap of waves against the boat.

'How's it going?'

'Rubbish, I can't get the beak right.'

I stand up to take a look, but then I glimpse something out the corner of my eye and it stops me in my tracks. For a moment there I could've sworn I saw the rod twitch. I stare at the tip, trying to discern whether the tiny movements are just the drag of the water on the line or a bite. Nothing. You can think you've seen a rod dip when it'll just be a trick of the light, but then again, yes, a definite tug this time. Billy's seen it too.

'Bite!' he shouts.

I put a hand on the shaft of the rod to steady it just as the reel starts spinning out.

'Is it a tunny?'

Best not get his hopes up. 'More likely a blue shark at that depth. They can get pretty big.'

Could be a tunny. The mackerel would've attracted more than gannets. Anyway, whatever it is, let him eat, don't take hold too quickly...

'He'll get away, Dad!'

'He's not going anywhere, son.'

The reel hisses as it spins out. He's taking a lot of line. I reach for the fight belt, quickly showing Billy how to help me tighten the straps. Once I've got the rod in my hands, I'll know what I've got. I take a breath and lock the reel, begin to take up the slack, yards and yards of it before I feel him. Then... *Jesus*.

'He's big.' I glance at Billy, see his own dark excitement, then I'm gabbling, thinking out loud. 'The line's deep, set it 60ft this time.'

'Catch him, Dad! Like Lorenzo.'

The hairs on the back of my neck bristle.

'Don't get your hopes up, Billy. Much more likely to be a shark, but hey, that'll still be something, won't it?'

I try to guess his weight, 40kg? 50kg? I'll treat him like a shark until

I know different. Give him some line, take it back, give it out. Wear him down. I feel him twist to the right and I yank up sharply on the rod, beads of water jumping from the line. Another two turns, just enough to let him know I won't let go.

You've got to let go, Tom.

I never liked that building, single storey, flat roofed. When it rained it sounded like a thousand tiny hammers. Impossible to think and yet they'd wait for me to say something – Anna and the counselor – looking at me as I stared out of the rain-flawed window. Our session was every Tuesday, same time as the community centre next door were holding their mother and baby group. I could hear them singing. *One, two, three, four, five, once I caught a fish alive...*

Billy leans over the side of the boat, hoping for a glimpse of the tunny. In his mind there's no doubt what it is. Won't see anything though, it's a long way out.

'How long until he gets tired?'

'Hours. If I fight him too soon, while he's still strong, he could snap the line.'

Billy yawns, but he's not bored now, just tired. He hasn't finished his sketch of the gannets, but he abandons it in favour of his kindle. In a few hours it'll be dark, and he'll be hungry again, but I can't rush this. The fish dictates the length of the fight and this one's pretty untroubled by me at the moment. I'm managing to hold him steady when he twists, but that's about it. Otherwise I'm not challenging him, or him me. I've got him now, that's all that matters. Just got to keep him.

An hour after the first star appears - a faint prick of light on a muddy pink canvas - darkness falls. Billy's asleep, curled up between the two benches, his head resting on the rucksack. I turn my attention back to the fish, which is a lot closer now, perhaps forty yards out, though it's hard to judge. I look for the line under the water, but the moon's turned the surface to glass.

I'm salted, sunburned, wildly excited and feeling like an idiot. We're long past the time I should've taken Billy back to Anna. She's not going to forgive this. As soon as I'd realized we weren't going to be back in time for dinner I'd phoned home and left a message on the answer machine, remembering too late that she wasn't there. Of course. We didn't live together anymore. I don't understand these jolts in memory, these skipped beats. I rang again, her mobile this time, and left a message as I try to do every night that he's with me. I said, truthfully, that he was sound asleep. I wasn't going to tell her we were on a boat far out at sea.

Why isn't the fish jumping? They always jump. Why isn't he trying to fight me? Surely that's hardwired into him, the determination to survive at any cost?

You've got to face up to what you're doing.

What am I doing? What I've always done. Put you first, put Billy first, that's all. That's all I've ever done.

The fish tugs, but he's getting weaker now. Perhaps he's ready to give in. I close my eyes; feel the boat's small movements, the weight of the rod in my hands. Something else, too, a beat. The fish's heart, or mine? *One, two, three, four, five, once I caught a fish alive...*

You've got to let him go.

Let him go? What, *now*? He's circling. This is it. I feel him veer to the left, a wide arc and then, for the first time, he turns towards me. I reel him in, nearer and nearer in an ever-decreasing circle. I'm closing in, but so is Anna.

Tom, he's gone.

What're you talking about? He's here, right here in front of me, and he's coming in fast. It's too dark to see him, but I can hear him, a great splash as he leaps. My heart leaps with him. I wait for him to come up again, but he doesn't, instead he goes deep, down into the dark where there's no light, no sound.

He leaps again and this time I see him, a flash of silver. As he falls, he twists and I see the ridges along his tail. He's not a shark. He's a *tunny*.

Look at me, Tom.

Not now, Anna. I go on reeling him in, closer to the boat. He glitters like a bright, blade under the water, full of light. I grab the harpoon, raise it high above my head. 'Billy, wake up! You've got to see this! You can't miss this. Billy?' I turn around, look for him, but he's not here. 'Billy, for God's sake...'

The space between the benches is empty. I scan the boat. He can't have gone overboard; I'd have heard the splash. The sketchpad's lying on the bench, open at a blank page. The sandwich I made him this morning hasn't been eaten, the bread's curling at the edges. The hot chocolate's beside it, the cup still full. It doesn't make any sense. I saw the drawing, I saw him eat.

He's gone. You've got to face up to it.

The fish tugs me back. He's lying on his side now next to the boat, looking up at me with a huge black eye, full of grief. He's no fight left in him. Blood smokes from his open mouth. I lower the harpoon. I know I can't kill him and so instead, I reach out and touch him. He's cold, dead cold, but beautiful. Always beautiful.

She's right. I've got to let you go, Billy.

I run my hand along his side, down as far as the golden ridges on his tail then I push my finger into his mouth and wrestle out the hook. At first, he doesn't seem to know he's free, he just floats there on the invisible thread that joins us. Then, I see a ripple move slowly down the length of his body and he starts to sink, a silver coin dropped in a well, falling away into the dark.

Sea Child

I WASN'T sure which came first, hearing the noise - a sharp yelp, followed moments later by a wind-like moan - or seeing the girl. Had she called out to me? I wondered how I hadn't seen her, suddenly there, where there'd been no one minutes before. From a distance she might've been a cloud shadow, advancing slowly across the sand, but then her body seemed to take shape and I saw that she was looking towards the dunes, a hand raised to pull a thick rope of hair from her eyes. She was small, skinny; nobody I knew.

Another yelp, louder this time. It was coming from somewhere near the tide line, but further along. The girl must've heard it too. This time it was unmistakable. An animal of some kind, had to be. I walked faster, listening, but only heard the waves, walls of chewed up sand that rose and crashed on the beach in seething arcs of foam.

'Did you hear that?'

I turned. She now stood only a few feet away from me.

'That noise,' she said.

'The wind.'

She wore a black swimsuit, peppered here and there with wet sand, and a thin, white cardigan. Pale legs and bare feet. She screwed up her eyes, scanning the beach behind us, her mouth slightly open. She had a gap where she'd lost a tooth. I tried to remember how long it was since I lost one.

I raked over a bit of bladderwrack with my foot, wanting her to go so I could see for myself what animal had made the noise, but she showed no sign of leaving.

'You from the campsite?' she asked.

'No.'

'We've got a van, me and me Dad.'

'I live in the house back there.'

'Maybe it was an owl,' she said, breathing out hard.

'They're quiet during the day, usually.'

She looked at me for what seemed like a long time, squinting because the sun, which had been rising steadily on the horizon, now met her eyes. She had a greenish bruise high on one cheekbone. We waited, both of us listening, but couldn't hear anything.

'Probably just a fox,' I said, knowing it wasn't.

'Did you find anything from the storm?' She nodded at the tide line. 'I saw you looking earlier.'

'Nah.'

'I did. Show you if you like. Come on.'

She turned and sprinted up the side of the nearest dune. At first, I only stared after her, wanting to stay on the beach in case I heard the noise again, but then I trotted after her, joining her halfway up the slope. She'd had to bend over to get her balance, bum up, and there were two pale circles of sand on the bony points of her bottom. At the top, she moved quickly along a narrow sandy path, leaping over clumps of spiky grass and then down into a clearing. Above us, the marram tossed in all directions. She walked across to a pile of clothes: a navy blue dress and sandals with large, white daisies stitched to the front. She waited for me to catch up and then crouched down, her swimsuit bunching up into wet ridges. Between her legs it'd ballooned into a pocket of air.

'The sea gave them me.' She pulled her clothes and sandals back to reveal a number of golden-skinned dolls, naked, plastic, wearing skimpy pink dresses - like Barbies except they looked Chinese with dark eyes and long, black hair.

'I had to wade in to get them - there were hundreds. I only got eight.'

She picked one up, adjusting its arm and placed it back on the sand. She'd arranged them all in funny positions, some on all fours, bums in the air, others lying on their backs with their legs pulled wide apart.

'Cool.'

She looked disappointed.

'A bomb got washed up here last summer,' I said quickly. 'From the war. Yeah, there'd been this big storm, like the one last night. They had to close the beach.'

Her eyes widened. 'Did it blow up?'

'No.'

'A roof came off one of the other vans, not ours though.' She sat back, digging two grooves in the sand for her heels to rest in. 'What's your name?'

'William.'

'I'm Bella, but soon as I'm old enough I'm changing it to Ruby.'

She offered no explanation for this, just stretched out onto the sand, flattening herself like she was sunbathing. I lay down too, sedge pricking my back. The sky was just beginning to clear but there was still a huge grey cloud above our heads with a hole in the middle, like a bruise healing.

'Dad says we're going home tomorrow,' she said. 'I've got school Monday.'

'Me too, only I'm going away.'

'Away?'

'Boarding school.'

'Won't you miss your friends?'

'A bit.'

I didn't want to tell her I didn't have any, or none I'd miss. Granddad, I'd miss him. The commode had changed things though, him having to go to the toilet right there in the living room, Mum helping, shouting when he didn't pull his pants down.

Bella was sitting up. She reached out and touched my forearm. 'All the hairs are sticking up. It's electricity, from the storm.'

She had it too; the skin on her legs was roughened by tiny bumps, and the hair on her head, the drier strands, lifting up and dancing. I caught a whiff of the sea's rot. We looked at each other and grinned.

'You can touch my fairy if you want.'

'What...?'

'My fairy. Don't you know what a fairy is?' She spread her legs and pointed to the mound.

'Give over.' I hoped I hadn't sounded rude. 'I mean just no. Thanks.'

'You're welcome.'

I sat up, bringing my knees to my chest. I'd not taken long to decide and none of the reasons I'd refused really worked on me. I tried to imagine what it'd feel like, the fleshy bud of a sea anemone perhaps.

'You're too young to be my girlfriend anyway.'

'You like me though, don't you? I can tell.'

I looked down at the patch of sand between my knees. 'I don't know you. We just met.'

'But I saw you watching me. You were – '

'Sshh!' I stood up, listened. A grunt, followed by a low-pitched groan. And again. Fainter. 'That noise again.'

We looked at each other, then Bella jumped to her feet and sprinted off ahead of me, back the way we'd come. I took a different route, hurling myself down a steep slope of sand, but we reached the beach at the same time and together we skipped into a jog, skidding to a halt when we couldn't hear it, setting off again as soon as there was another cry. I was sure it was coming from the tide line, but where? The cove played tricks with sound; far away things could seem much nearer than they were. I shut my eyes and listened hard but heard only the waves breaking and the soft hiss as they spread along the beach.

When I opened my eyes I was surprised to find that Bella had moved some distance to my right which I was sure was the wrong direction. A gust of wind stippled my legs with sand followed immediately by a lull, like a breath held. Then, a terrible cry. I thought one of Jensen's calves must've escaped and got stuck somewhere, but the farm was a mile away at least. I set off at a sprint, faster than Bella then at the tide line I stopped and edged along it. There were the usual fronds of salt-rimed kelp, a tangle of dark knots that might've been netting, bone-white driftwood, a chair leg, but I looked only for signs of movement. And then I saw it. An eye - wet, shining - opened and then closed again. I crouched down and Bella dropped to her knees beside me, breathing heavily.

It was a seal, a pup.

Immediately he flared his nostrils and tried to get away, but part of a fishing net was wound around him. He was young, silver-grey, with darker spots dappling his throat and underside, and huge, liquid-brown eyes. He smelled sweet, briny - something else too, metallic. Blood. I leant closer and saw that the net was cutting deep into his tail.

Bella reached out to touch him.

'Don't,' I said. 'He might bite.'

At the sound of my voice the pup's nostrils flared.

'Poor thing.'

'Something'll find him before long.'

'Like what?'

'A fox maybe.'

'We have to help him. Cover him up.'

'No point if he keeps shouting like that.'

'Lift him then, take him back to the sea.'

'The blood will attract predators.'

'Sharks?'

I shrugged. I didn't know if there were any round here, not for sure. The kindest thing would probably be to hit him over the head with a rock but that was easy to say. I knew I wouldn't be able to do it. I could hear the tears in Bella's voice, her sharp, fast breaths as she tried to hold them back. The pup opened his wide mouth, long whiskers bunching together as he gave a silent cry.

'The fishermen must've seen him and cut him loose without bothering to free him,' I said.

'They should've helped him.'

'Not as easy as that.'

I could see the pup's tiny white teeth and his tongue, pink and rough with barbs.

Bella touched my arm. 'We have to get the net off. Look around, there might be something to cut it with.'

'We really shouldn't try. There's no point.'

She wasn't listening. She moved up the tide line, dropped to her knees and began clawing back clumps of bladderwrack with her hands. Sand flies dotted the air around her and now and then she spat when one got in her mouth.

Cautiously, I took hold of a piece of the netting and tugged it, but the pup swung around for my wrist.

'There's nothing here,' she said, sounding desperate. 'I'll go back to the van, get a knife.'

'*No.*'

She freed her eyes from hair, looked at me.

'I told you, there's no point. Even if we get him loose, he won't survive.'

'We've got to do *something.*'

'You're not responsible for him, you know? It's nature, this kind of thing happens.' I hated myself for saying it. I sounded just like my father. 'Pups don't know to steer clear of the boats. They try to steal fish from the nets.'

I could see she didn't care *why* it'd happened. She only wanted to save him. She strode quickly back over to the pup, frantic now, trying to grab a thread of net, losing it, grabbing it again. She began sawing a strand with the serrated edge of a clam shell, but it wasn't sharp enough. Her knees were bleeding, scratched from kneeling on the broken shells and driftwood that were mixed in with the seaweed.

'Bella – '

'It's not working.' She started to get up. 'We need a knife.'

I put a hand on her arm, but she pulled away from me.

'What's wrong with you? Why won't you help? We need a *knife.*'

'Please. Just wait a minute.'

I lifted the tip of his tail to look at the cut, hoping it wouldn't be as bad as I thought, but the pup lurched forward again making a throaty screeching sound.

She lashed at my arm. 'You're hurting him!'

I didn't know why I wanted to stop her going back to the campsite to get the knife. Nothing to do with the pup, which I was sure would die no matter what we did. I suppose I was afraid she'd come back with her Dad, or someone, and I didn't want that. I wanted it to be just us, as it'd been in the dunes before we'd found him, sealed in by the marram whipping on the tops above our heads, the electricity of the storm pricking our skin.

'You really care about him, don't you?' I said.

'*Yes.*'

'All right.' I moved around so that I was directly behind the pup, leaning over him so I could get a better look at the netting. It'd be possible, just, to get it off without cutting it, but it'd mean my grabbing him and holding him still long enough for her to free his tail.

'I think it'll come loose but you'll have to do it because I'll have to keep his head still in case he tries to bite.'

She looked shocked, paler now.

'Do you think you can?'

No answer.

She was right, of course, the knife would do it in seconds and so I felt I was tricking her in a way, making her believe we could do it ourselves. The pup tried to lift his head again, but he'd no strength left. Slowly, she put her hand in front of his mouth. I reached out to stop her, frightened he'd snap at her, but he didn't move.

'He's getting weaker,' she said. 'Come on then. Let's try.'

I shuffled around to the side of the pup, glancing now and then at Bella. The hollow at the bottom of her neck was tinged almost yellow and she'd sucked in her bottom lip.

In one swift move, I put my knee on the back of the pup's head, pressing down with all my weight, but immediately he started thrashing and I lost my balance and fell back on to the sand. He eyed me, panting. I knew I had to try again and so this time I used my hands as well, shouting at Bella to hurry. I could see her wrestling with the netting, she'd got a bit of it over the end of his tail, but there was still more. Her fingers were covered in blood.

'There's just one more bit,' she said, gasping. 'I think I can get it on the next go.'

The pup was wailing, making it difficult to hear her. He beat his tail up and down, panicked, sprayed us with sand and blood. A drop shot up and landed on my neck. I wanted us to leave him. We were doing more harm than good, and it was all my fault because I should've let her get the knife. I looked at her, her chest puffing in and out, her ribs visible through her swimsuit.

'Ready,' she said.

I grabbed the pup again, my fingers digging into his fur as I pressed down with all my weight. I glanced at Bella. She was bent over the netting, picking at a strand of it, loosening a knot, dropping it each time he moved, then trying to find it again. I looked at the pup's head, pinned, its nostrils pink and flared with pain and fear. It was still for only a few seconds, but then started wailing and writhing under me again.

A shout from Bella. 'There!'

I let go, staggering back, and collided with her. Breathless, we fell on the sand beside the pup.

A laugh burst out of me. 'You did it!'

I turned to her and buried my head in her neck, my mouth open, the

70

smell of her filling my nose: sea rot, mixed with the fainter sweetness of her sweat.

'I thought it'd never come off,' she said. 'Look at me, his blood's all over my hands.'

'Me too, I got a bit.'

She laughed, lifting the hem of her cardigan to wipe a smear off my cheek.

'We could look for a pool,' I said. 'Wash it off.'

'What about him?'

'He'll be all right, reckon we should let him calm down a bit anyway. He's pretty angry.'

Long tongues of sea water had swelled around the basalt rocks to form deep pools. Bella ran towards one and crouched down to dip her hands in.

'I could go and get a towel,' she said.

'We'll soon dry off.'

'No, I mean we could use it to drag the pup down to the sea.'

'The tide's coming in now. He'll be all right.'

'OK.'

She grinned, splashed me and then jumped up, shrieking, as I scooped up water with both hands and chucked it at her. I wanted to hold her, but she was never still, not for a minute, until, at last, she spun around in front of me, losing balance and I caught her.

'I feel drunk,' she said.

'You're just dizzy. It was amazing, you know? What you did.'

She kissed me then, planting her cold lips on mine, not moving, though I could feel her eyelashes on my cheek. It was over quickly. I tasted my lips, a sugary fizz that pricked in my groin and made the hairs on the back of my neck stand up.

'What did you do that for?' I said, half laughing.

'Don't you feel it? Electricity.'

Then she spun away from me, swinging back a second later to grab my hand. Slowly, we walked back to the pup. I was surprised to find he'd struggled a few yards down the beach. The tide was racing in now. Once the waves reached him, he'd move more easily and so we waited, sat some distance away. He wouldn't understand that we'd tried to help him, Bella said, but one day he'd thank us. I didn't think he'd survive the night, but I didn't say so. Bella was so proud of what we'd done, that we'd saved him.

And maybe we had. I wanted to believe we had.

I shall go into a hare
With sorrow and sighing and mickle care

Rain Hare

A BULLISH spring wind came first, hours before the rain, but then I saw the black belly of cloud in the distance and moved the ewes into the barn. By mid-afternoon the storm reached us, a sudden darkness like a lid closing; then it began to pour. It rained steadily into that night and through the next day and the next until I couldn't remember when it had begun and each day started and ended the same. At times, it drummed on my back for hours, but mostly it was a mizzling, melancholic rain that drained the land of colour and seeped through my clothes. Tongues of water ran the length of the fields and the troughs and ditches overflowed and made watery graves for anything that tried to grow. Worst of all, was its chatter - incessant, nagging - that pursued me as I went about my work: the trickle from the farmhouse gutter, the pelt on the barn roof, the whispery thud on dry straw. Even when it stopped, my brain still carried the sound of it, an endless *drip, drip, drip.*

Now, at last, I stood on the yard, palms turned up to the sky and felt not a drop. My first thought was to wake Clare and tell her it was over, but, no, I'd let her sleep. Max was bounding about, his nose a compass for the scents released by the rain. I scraped my hair into a ponytail and went to check on the ewes. They waddled over to me, fat with their lambs, but none looked ready, so I turned Flint out into the paddock, his great hooves kicking up splatters of mud as he trotted away; then I walked up Hill Field. I'd been hoping the ditch would hold, but before I'd halfway reached it, I could see water coming over the rim, a dull mud-coloured stream that puddled around the hayrack.

Only weeks ago, I'd climbed into that ditch, crouched down, peering over the top, and waited with my gun for the fox. It was a sign of how much the grey, wet days had got to me that I'd not even looked for him. I knew his earth was somewhere in the long stretch of Bankfoot wood, but I saw only the trunks of the firs now, copper bright in the sun. He'd be there though, twining in and out of the trees, pausing now and then with a paw raised, to look down on the farm.

I could shore up the ditch with sand bags, but what we really needed was a long dry spell. Turning back to the farmhouse, I saw Lower and Well Field and the copse of oak running between them. Together with Hill Field and the wood, the farm amounted to forty acres, a mere finger of land compared to the neighbouring steads, but more than enough work for me.

'Here, Max!'

I set off to take a look at the fallen oak, Max bounding through the trench mud at the gate ahead of me and then, when he reached the tree, leaping onto its trunk. The air was heavy, moist, but the sky was pale and clear. The oak had uprooted rather than broken, leaving a shell hole in the earth and damage to the fence; a whole section would need to be replaced. God knows when I'd have the time or money to fix it.

I was about to turn back up the field when a movement in the long grass caught my eye. Max, having picked up the scent, circled twice, then he was off at a trot. A rabbit, likely; he got one most mornings. Once he'd spotted it, he'd bolt away on one of his chases and I'd not see him for hours, but now he was still sniffing about doubtfully and I saw it a second before he did. Not a rabbit. A hare. It'd got caught in the barbed wire and lay, trapped, eyes bulging, nostrils flared. Wounded. Max lunged, heckles up, his barks thinned to a squeak; then I heard his growl and I knew he'd got his teeth on it.

'Leave!'

I yanked him back, though he continued to lunge at the air, choking himself on his collar. I tethered him to a branch of the oak and returned to the hare, thinking he might've killed it, but it was just lying very still, its quick, shallow breaths the only sign of life. A jill probably, jacks were smaller. Clare'd know. I reached forward to pull back some stalks of grass for a better look. Gawky thing, but that flaming iris - beautiful. I'd not seen one up close, not alive anyway, mostly I'd see them startled, zipping this way and that; sometimes I found tufts of their fawny fur scattered about. This one lay flat on her side, her large, unblinking eyes fixed on mine. Probably been trapped a while. I examined the cut made by the wire; deep and on the fleshy part of her thigh. The leg wasn't broken, though she'd be slower on it, easy prey. Really, I ought to let Max finish her; at least it'd be quick, yet I hesitated, thinking of Clare. She liked painting hares most of all. She'd want the jill saved, taken back to the house to see what, if anything, could be done.

I found my pocketknife and pulled out the pair of clippers. They were small, fiddly, but I got them around the wire and managed to snip through it in two places. Sensing freedom, the hare began to strike out with her powerful hind limbs, and before I could grab her scruff, she wrenched free, a single giant arc, and sprinted across the field. Damn it. She kicked up divots of wet mud, veered right, twisting as she caught sight of Max at the oak and skidding onto her side, the weakened leg not bearing her weight, but then she righted herself and bolted through the copse into Lower Field.

Max was panting, yelping with excitement. Should've let him have her. *Stupid.* Now she'd suffer. Still, it was too late now. I went back to the ewe shed, gave them fresh hay and then returned to the farmhouse, pausing at the gate to see if I could get another glimpse of the hare, but she'd long gone.

I heeled off my boots on the porch and went into the kitchen. Clare wasn't there as she usually was, nor were the breakfast things laid out on the table.

'Clare?'

One of her headaches perhaps; she often got them so bad she could do nothing but lie in a dark room and wait for them to pass. I'd find her there sometimes, cheeks bone-white and a film of sweat across her forehead. I took the loaf from the bin and two hard-boiled eggs from the larder, looked for the jam, but couldn't find it. Clare had her own way of keeping things. As I sat at the table, I heard her bedroom door open and a few moments later she appeared, hands scrabbling behind her back to tie her pinny.

'There you are,' I said.

'It's stopped raining, I see.' She placed the kettle on the stove and pulled down the teapot from the shelf, pressing a hand to one hip and wincing as she set cups on the counter.

'I thought you must have one of your headaches.'

'No.'

She sat at the table beside me, cut a slice from the loaf.

'But you're all right?'

'Yes, don't fuss.' She glanced at me, hesitating before she added: 'Fell over in the mud, didn't I? Feeding the hens. I had to change.'

I took another mouthful of bread to stifle my laugh.

'Oh, go on, *laugh*. I hope it's the last of the rain, I tell you, don't know how much more of it I can stand.'

'Did you hurt yourself?'

'I'll live.' She buttered her bread, stealing one of the eggs from my plate to peel. 'How's Hill Field looking?'

'Flooded. Ditch'll need some work when the water's drained off a bit, Flint'd get up there now probably, but there's no point 'till it's dried up.'

'Forecast is for sun with a risk of showers - if we're unlucky.'

I poured the tea, wanting to tell her about the hare, but it'd only upset her. I looked at the painting above the hearth, a hare so life-like it seemed about to leap into the room. It was her best and so, ignoring her protests, I'd insisted she hang it there. Clare cut up her egg, but instead of eating it she pushed her plate away and took a gulp of tea, elbows on the table, the mug cupped in her hands. She looked tired, her big eyes scarcely blinking.

'Are you sure you're all right? I could look at your leg?'

'I'm perfectly fine.'

'Okay...I went to take a look at the oak. It's a good ten yards of fencing that needs replacing.'

'But only into the copse. The sheep won't mind getting in there.'

'Getting them out again - that'll be the bother. Max is no sheep dog.'

Clare tore off a corner of bread and dropped it on the floor for him then looked at my plate. 'Sorry you've not had a hot breakfast. I'll do a stew for tonight, if you like?'

'That'd be nice.' I noticed the buttons on her blouse were done up in the wrong order. 'Angus's coming over to talk about the shoot.'

'I thought they'd finished?'

'He added another. He'll give us the numbers today.'

She stared into her mug. 'Lot of trouble just to come over for that. He could telephone.'

'Clare, please.'

'Right.' She stood up, limped across to the sink. 'Well, you'll need to bring me a rabbit and a couple of chickens. You can kill that cock too while you're at it, he's no good for the girls and he fights with Russell.'

'You shouldn't give them names.'

'I don't. Only him.'

'I could put Angus off for today if you're not up to it?'

'I said I was fine.' She stared out of the kitchen window, her hands briskly washing a mug. 'Doesn't bother me anyway. It's you he's after.'

'He is not!'

I said it lightly, but I was nettled. Her dislike of him was becoming a problem. She took her plate, not meeting my eyes, and scraped her uneaten breakfast into the bin.

'You know without Angus's shoots we'd be even more hard up than we are.'

'Have I complained? Not once. Not even when I found one of them relieving himself on the side of the hen house.'

What did it matter? Six days a year, it was nothing. Even with all the cooking, it wasn't too much to ask. 'He's only ever helped us. It wouldn't hurt you to -' I saw her take a breath. 'What?'

'The way he looks at you, Faye. You must know - practically salivating.'

'Not a crime.'

'Not if you've sense to stay clear.'

'I don't encourage him.'

She turned the tap on so hard it splashed water up to her face, then she just stood, breathing. 'Well, as long you don't go and do anything silly.'

'Ha! I don't have time to be silly. I'm out there, getting soaked, feeding and shoveling muck and... Oh, never mind.'

Clare snatched the tea towel off the rail and wiped her cheek with it.

'Anyway, Angus said he'd help -'

'Did I hear someone say my name?'

We turned, both of us startled. Angus stood in the doorway.

'I did knock,' he said, removing his cap and running a hand through his hair. His eyes, quick and soft, cast me a glance.

Clare edged away from the sink, busied herself clearing out the grate. She'd flushed, with fright or embarrassment, I didn't know which.

'Tea, Angus?' I said. 'The kettle's on and Clare looks to be setting the fire.'

'I won't say no, still a nip in the air. Clare,' he nodded at her as she turned around, but she met his eyes only briefly. 'Lots of compliments from the last shoot on your roast chicken, the sauce, what you baste it in, right treat they said.'

She looked at him again, her eyes wide. 'Good.'

'I expect you'll be glad to get the ewes out, Faye?'

'Yes, though the fields are a mess.'

He smiled, passing his cap back and forth between his hands. The gesture seemed childish, nervous, though he was a confident man.

'Come and sit down, Clare,' I said. 'And you, Angus. I'll make us all a pot of tea, or do you want coffee?'

'I'll have what you're both having,' Clare said. 'Save me being a nuisance.'

'You're not, don't be daft.'

Clare sat at the hearth end, the painting of the hare above her. Angus chose the chair opposite. I could see he was trying to think of something to say to her, but she made no effort, instead picking up the knitting she ordinarily did in the evenings and beginning a new row. The kettle simmered quietly.

'So, the shoot, next month, the 29ᵗʰ, isn't it?' I said.

'That's right, be our biggest yet, I reckon. Still a few more to firm up, but I think we'll be looking at sixteen all in. I'll bump up what I give you, of course, it'll be a lot of food.' He looked at Clare. 'I expect they'll be happy with whatever you do.'

'Rabbit, chicken, the trimmings.' The clicking of needles paused for a second or two, though she didn't look up. 'Just like always.'

'Right,' Angus said.

'They won't want for anything.'

'Perhaps a hare?' he said.

Clare looked to me, to him.

'Used to do a nice jugged hare me nanna did.' He had a smear of a grin on his face now, a taunting, mocking glint in his eyes. He leaned back in his chair, legs apart. 'No matter, chicken's fine, that's if you've still got any. Not got that fox yet, Faye? Don't see his brush on the door.'

'Not yet.' His eyes followed me across the room. 'Don't you get him on the shoot either, I want him.'

'You don't mean that, Faye,' Clare said, startled. 'I know he's a bother, but you sound like you'd take pleasure in killing him.'

'Too right,' Angus said.

'I don't take pleasure in it. I meant that I wanted it to be me, that's all.'

But she was looking at Angus, wide-eyed and silent, hands poised and tense on the needles. He blew on his tea, top lip curled back as he took a sip; then, when he looked up, I saw again that glint of mischief. He liked to play Clare, but it was only a bit of teasing. I thought nothing of it - he'd all the charm and innocence of a little boy caught looking up a girl's skirts – but I could see it rattled her.

'I'll take this upstairs if that's all the arranging that needs doing for the shoot,' she said.

Angus waited until she'd left the room and then let a stream of air out through his lips. 'By God, she's stiff.'

'*Angus.*'

'What? Talks like an old maid and what is she, forty?'

'Not as old as that.'

'Then why's she not out there with you helping on the farm? She lives off you and what do you get in return?'

'She paints, that brings in a bit.'

Angus was looking at the hare painting, an expression of amusement on his face. He stood up and moved around the table until he was beneath it. 'What they sell for then? Can't imagine Boyles takes that many.'

'When will you have the final numbers?' I said, opening the ledger where I kept details of the shoots.

'Never could work out what it is about this one. Now I see it, it's the eyes. They look human.'

I looked at the hare again. They did, in a way, though I'd not noticed it before. I turned to a clean page, but he moved to the back of my chair and leaned over.

'When we going to get together, Faye?'

I could feel his breath on the side of my neck, a hotness that felt almost like pain. 'Don't, Angus.'

His hands cupped my shoulders, then, just briefly, he let his lips brush against my skin, and I felt again that searing heat. I ducked away, but he didn't linger, returning to his chair. His eyes were clear, penetrating; whenever he looked at me, I felt it as a knowing.

'You didn't answer me,' he said.

'I don't know what you mean.' He reached for my hand, but I pulled it away. 'Anyway, I want to ask you something.'

'Ask me anything.'

'The oak, the one that came down in the storm last month? You said you'd help me clear it.'

'Oh, *that*.' He sighed deeply, stretching his arms above his head. 'Course, I'll get lend of a tractor and bring some lads down, have it done in an afternoon.'

'I can't give you anything for it.'

'Faye, I told you I'd do it.' He flicked a crumb off the table, a crease appearing on his forehead. 'I don't like to see you struggling.'

'I keep my end up at the market, don't I?'

'Course you do.'

I wasn't convinced he thought so. It mattered to me to do at least as well as the men, even though I knew success at farming was as much luck as anything else. I set down the pencil on the ledger and folded my arms.

'It's just a lot for one person, Faye, one pair of hands. You need someone with you.'

'I can't afford a labourer.'

'I'll help out more, once the season's over.'

'No. Besides, you've got that job on Keith Patrick's farm, haven't you? Harvesting.'

'Still gives me a couple of months sitting on my backside - might as well be you looking at it.'

I smiled then. Swiftly, he pulled me up, pressing me against the sink. 'Be*have!*'

But he was grinning, his small white teeth shining with spit. 'I know you want me, I know you do.'

He slid his arms around my waist, dodging my half-hearted attempts to claw them away and then he kissed my neck. Why didn't I give myself to him? It wouldn't be difficult. I breathed him in, his smell, almost feral, of pine needles, wood and earth.

I pushed him back. 'Clare's upstairs.'

'So?'

I moved away, curling loose strands of hair behind my ears.

'You need her permission?'

'No-o.'

'Aw, c'mon, Faye.' The skin around the collar of his shirt had flushed brick-red. I thought he might storm out, but he just stood, took his cap from the table and lowered his eyes.

'If you heard half of what people are saying... Just as well I know different, Faye.'

'What?'

'There's talk.'

'There's always talk.' I was a favourite topic amongst the farmers' wives. 'I don't care to hear it.'

'Perhaps you should.' He hesitated. 'Clare does you no favours.'

'Oh, don't start *that* again.'

'What they supposed to think? They see her about the village, darting in and out of shops like a frightened rabbit, doesn't talk to anyone. And that business with her Dad's farm over in Leigh.'

'What about it?'

'The young woman that killed herself.'

What young woman? Clare'd not mentioned anyone. I busied myself turning pages of the ledger. 'What of it?'

'Davey Fenshaw delivered beet up there, says the lass was only there a year with Clare and her Dad, but they were definitely together – a couple.'

'Well, Clare's mother died when she was a child. He'd be free to -'

'No, not him, *Clare*. Her and the woman, a couple. You know... lovers.'

Laughter burst from me.

'It's true, Faye.'

'Davey Fenshaw's a drunk!'

'He's not a liar.'

'I've better things to do than listen to wagging tongues.'

He looked at me, searching my eyes even when I tried to look away. 'Clare's not told you about her, has she?'

'I have to get on, Angus.'

'Do you know *anything* about her?' He shook his head, disbelieving. 'Doesn't it matter to you that –'

'Let me know when you can do the oak.'

I wanted him gone. Nonsense, all of it. Gossip. Those women wanted us out, they'd say anything. Wanted me to fail as they'd said all along I would. Well, I wasn't going to give them the satisfaction.

Angus had put on his cap, but I didn't look at him. I was angry with him for telling me, angry too that he seemed to think it true. He moved to kiss me and when I resisted, he put two fingers under my chin and raised it. I expected to see anger, but what I saw wasn't that, something kinder.

'I don't like to see you being made a fool of.'

He rubbed my cheek with his thumb, smoothing off a bit of muck I'd not known was there, then kissed me lightly.

I didn't want him, which made no sense of the queer effect he had on me. I listened to his car pulling away down the lane and then it was quiet again. A few minutes later I heard Clare moving about upstairs, but I put my boots back on and went out onto the yard. The hens were pecking at the seed in the pen, the cock strutting between them, upsetting their metronomic rhythm. I felt a drop of rain on my cheek.

The rest of the morning I kept myself busy outside. When I called in at the house at midday there was a note from Clare. *Gone into the wood to pick garlic. Sandwich in the larder.* I wrapped the sandwich up and took it out with me. The ewes were skittish from so long inside so I had to dart about, banging my stick on the ground to shoo them into Lower Field. By the time they were all in and I'd closed the gate I was hot and out of breath. I removed my jumper and rolled up my sleeves, perching on the gatepost to eat my lunch. A badger was shuffling along, tempted out of the copse in daylight by the easy pickings of drowned earthworms.

I'd tried to put what Angus told me out of my mind, but it followed me around, needling its way in as I went about my jobs. What nobody could fathom, what nobody understood, was how much I owed her. It didn't matter that she was nervous of the animals and prone to bouts of illness. She was good at keeping the farmhouse; we always ate well. When last Spring she'd come asking about a room in exchange for housekeeping, it made perfect sense to me, not just because I was too tired in the evenings to do anything much for myself, but because before Clare, on those painfully lonely winter evenings I'd had nothing, nothing but silence and the endless weight of darkness. Clare in love with a girl? I'd *know* if she was that way. I knew her.

The afternoon remained sunny and dry, the threatening clouds over the hills gradually shifting away on the breeze and as I walked back to the farmhouse at dusk I felt happier than I'd done for a long time. I fetched some more logs from the store, clutching them against my chest as I opened the door.

'Wow, smells great,' I said.

Clare was standing at the stove, stirring the contents of a pot. When she saw me, she came over and took the logs from me one at a time, dropping them into the basket by the hearth.

'Are you done?' she asked.

'But for the ewe checks. I reckon they're all planning to drop in one night, the little blighters.'

'I'll come out with you if they do.'

She limped back to the chopping board and took up a handful of wild garlic.

'You should've taken it easy if your leg's still bothering you.'

'I wanted us to have a good meal. There are some celandines out, primroses, too. I thought of picking some, but I think I'll wait for the bluebells.'

I peeled off my socks and put them in the basket in the washroom while she ladled out two bowlfuls of stew. She handed me a torn off hunk of bread and we ate in our chairs by the fire.

'It's a treat to still have the fire, isn't it?' Clare said. 'It's not too warm.'

'No, it's nice.'

After we'd finished, I offered to wash up, but she told me to leave it and so we sat back, our feet together on the foot stool. My eyes began to feel heavy, but I kept trying to stretch them open, knowing it'd be fatal to nod off before the ewe checks were done.

'Play something?' I asked.

'That'll really put you to sleep.'

'It won't.'

She pulled the side table in front of her and laid her ukelin across it. Odd looking thing, a cross between a violin and a ukulele. The sound was as haunting as it was beautiful. I watched her hands move over the instrument, one on the bow, the other plucking the strings with thin, pale fingers. She'd been given it by her father, hadn't she? Yes, he'd found it in an antique shop and she'd taught herself to play. She must've played it for him. And the woman? Had Clare played for her too? I pushed the thought away, but it got larger in my mind, a pressure growing between the notes. By the time she'd finished the piece it was as though I'd conjured the woman with all my thinking. She was with us in the room.

Clare began turning the pegs one at a time, strumming the strings to check the sound.

'Do you ever wish you were married?' I asked.

'What an odd question.' She looked into the fire before raising her eyes to me. 'You must wish it for yourself to ask such a thing.'

'I suppose I always imagined I would be by now.'

She set the ukelin down and leant back in her chair to gaze into the flames. I could see them in her eyes, tiny slivers of orange.

'I don't see what you'd gain from it,' she said, quietly. 'You have land of your own and...'

I waited.

'Company, in me. If I don't irritate you too much.'

'You don't.' I looked at her. 'I'd be lost without you.'

She seemed taken aback.

'Ah, c'mon. You know I would.'

She smiled into the fire, her eyes glazed with tears.

'Don't cry, you idiot.'

'I'll do no such thing.' She kicked off her slippers and put her feet again with mine on the stool. 'You remind me of someone, your sense of humour.'

'Who?'

'Oh,' she rubbed her nose, 'just someone I knew.'

'Who?'

'A woman. A friend. It was a long time ago.'

'In Leigh?' I stared at her, waiting. 'On your father's farm?'

She shot me a glance. 'Your face, Faye, you've gone quite serious.'

'Have I? I just wondered, you've not talked much about your life before here. What happened to her?'

'I don't know.'

A lie. She put the ukelin away and when she returned to her chair she drew her legs up beside her and resumed her knitting, the corners of her mouth twitching as if in some urgent conversation with herself. I watched her for a time, thinking how I might approach the subject again, but the moment had passed. I felt worse for having exposed her lie and now it stretched between us, a distance where there'd not been one before. I picked up my book, but I couldn't focus on the words and an hour or so passed with me reading the same few pages over and over. I must've let my eyes close for I felt myself drifting somewhere between sleep and waking, listening to the seethe and crackle of the fire, the click-click of her needles, and at the edges, perhaps even in a dream, the distant bark of the fox.

A few days later, Angus turned up to tackle the oak, a chainsaw in the boot of his car, but none of the lads were with him who he'd said would help. He said they were all busy working other farms, but I suspected he hadn't asked. Clare'd gone to Boyles and so the two of us went together to the tree.

'How's lambing, Faye?'

'Two last night.'

'Straight forward?'

'One was a stillborn, first-timer.' I lifted the latch on the gate and let him through ahead of me.

'You always lose a few.'

'Yes.'

He strode briskly down the field and it was as much as I could do to keep up with him. Now and then he threw a stick for Max, too big for him to carry, but he dragged it back each time. He was jumping around Angus's feet, getting in the way of his walking.

'Max!'

'He's all right.'

He lay down the chainsaw and wrestled the stick from Max's mouth, almost lifting him off the ground, then he leant back and hurled the stick as far as he could. Max shot away. 'I was thinking, why don't I stay here on the farm with you, just until lambing's over?'

'I can manage.'

'What happens if you've got two lambing at the same time and there's a problem? Always is with lambs.'

'Clare can help.'

He looked doubtful. 'She's done it before, has she?'

'I can manage.'

I walked on to the tree. We were silent for a time, but I could tell he was worried about me. Perhaps my tiredness had begun to show. I'd not made much of an effort with myself, my hair loosely tied in a bun. He examined the fencing and pulled out the damaged planks.

'I've got more in the back of the barn,' I said. 'I'll bring them down.'

'Clear this lot first, I reckon the bulk of it Flint can pull up.'

'I thought you'd got lend of a tractor?'

'*You* should have a tractor.'

'They cost money.' I sat on the trunk, watched him pull off the smaller twigs and branches and toss them in a pile. The thicker ones he had to snap over his knee. It was clouding over, a thick belt of black casting a shadow over the copse.

'You know how many farms there are still using horses?'

'I expect you'll tell me.'

He shook his head, smiling. 'Just telling you how it is.'

'I know.'

'You could see about a loan, maybe look at taking Burridge's old pasture across the road. Get yourself some Herefords or Aberdeens, you'd sharp pay it off. Sheep'll not turn a decent profit with the numbers you got.'

'You've thought about it a lot.'

He shrugged, standing on a particularly stubborn branch and pulling up sharply on one end to break it. He gave me a sidelong glance. 'Don't be thinking you're lady of the manor, mind, sitting there on your backside while the cheap labour works.'

'*Free* labour.'

'I could feel taken advantage of.'

I smiled. 'You'd like nothing more no doubt.'

He put on his gloves and lifted up the chainsaw, pulling the cord until it stirred into a roar. He started on the thicker branches first, cutting them where they joined the trunk then I pulled them free and dragged them a distance away ready to get a rope on. Once it was just the main trunk that was left, he switched off the saw, wiping an arm across his forehead then biting down on the fingers of his gloves to pull them off.

'I could run up to the house, get us a drink?'

He pulled off his shirt, just his vest underneath. A flash of furred belly. I looked away, not quick enough, for when I glanced at him again he was smiling.

'Sit here a while with me,' he said.

'I should get the planks.'

'C'mon.'

We sat on the trunk and looked down the field. It was warm, despite the clouds, and the drying fields had sweetened the air with the smell of new grass.

'You know I like you, Faye, we joke around, but I do.'

'I don't -'

'Here we go. Bit of a habit you brushing me off.'

'It's not like that. It's...' I drew myself up. All my excuses sounded worn. It was nice, the two of us working, joking around. 'It takes all of me to run this place, Angus, I've nothing left to give.'

'So let me help you out a while? I'll sleep in a chair, Jesus, I'll sleep in the barn if you like. At least consider it.'

I hesitated. 'I'll need to talk to Clare.'

'Why?'

'Because it's her home too.'

He turned his head away and spat into the grass. 'Not her farm though, is it?'

'She knows that.'

'Does she? Seems to me you don't even know who you're living with.'

I sighed heavily.

'No, just listen. I've seen the way -'

'I don't *care*.'

'I've seen the way she looks at you. You must know, Faye.'

It started to rain, a few spots at first, but soon it was a deluge, thick rods that struck the oak and trickled around its girth. Angus grabbed the saw and took shelter in the copse. 'Come under here.'

I lifted my face to the rain; feeling it on my lids, feeling it flatten my hair. It wasn't true, he was wrong.

'Faye, you're soaked, for Chris'sake.'

Clare didn't love me, not like that. He came to stand beside me, his hair darkening in the rain.

'She's got secrets.' He took hold of my arm. 'What secrets you got, eh?'

'None.'

'No?'

I pushed him away and marched back up the field. The rain was heavy on my head, falling so thickly I could barely make out the shape of the house and wood behind. I slid on the mud; my boots cement heavy. Angus was shouting after me, but I couldn't make out the words.

Once back at the house, I took up the log basket to fill it, but quickly changed my mind, thinking I'd clear the drain next to the barn instead and so went to the shed to find something to prise open the cover. Rain, deafening, beating on the roof, clawing at the window like it wanted to be inside. I couldn't breathe, not there, not back on the yard either, everywhere seemed too small for how I felt. In the end, I fetched my gun from the porch.

By the time I reached Bankfoot the rain had slowed to a drizzle and the sun was beginning to splinter through the clouds. Several rooks who'd been waiting for the shower to pass erupted from the trees and circled the field, landing in twos and threes to pick for worms. I turned away from them and stepped into the shadowy dimness of the wood. Cool air from the darkness further in reached me, but I remained close to the edge, moving slowly, stepping over the ruin of an old tree thickly studded with lichen. I wanted to stay where I could see the farm and from here, I could see it all, the yard and the two fields below it, the copse and the fallen oak.

Angus wasn't there, nor anywhere I could see. His car was still on the yard though. Then I saw him. He was with Clare on the lane. I could clearly make out Angus's white vest and Clare's blue velvet cap, but I was too far away to hear what they were saying or read their faces. Clare, rigid, stood in front of Angus who had his hands on his hips. What could they find to talk about for so long? But talking, not arguing, no, but then he jabbed a finger into her face and she stepped sharply to one side. A terrible fear overcame me. I started to run back the way I'd come, slipping near the ditch at the top of the field. I swore, skating the mud as I struggled to my feet, looked again, but it was already over, Angus striding back to the oak, Clare going onto the yard. I stood a while, panting, not knowing what to do or where to be, then, slinging my gun across my shoulder, I turned and walked deep into the wood.

It took a long time, but eventually I found the fox's earth and waited nearby, tucked into a nest of brambles. There, with only the quiet breathing of the wood, the farm seemed distant. Just me and the fox. Once or twice I was convinced I could smell him, a deeply feral odour reaching me on a breath, but he didn't show himself.

When I returned, I looked for Angus's car. Gone. I went to the barn and, to my horror, found a ewe in the last stage of labour. She'd lain down with her back to a bale, quiet, only the occasional bleat at the peak of a contraction. I should've been with her. I hung back, watched and waited, then - the ewe struggling to her feet – I saw the lamb's head crown and seconds later a liquid puddle dropped to the straw. Immediately, the mother began to lick the sac. I waited until the lamb was on its feet and nuzzling then went back to the house. Clare was sitting by the fire.

'I was starting to worry,' she said.

'No need.'

'You've been gone hours. And the state of you, where've you been?'

'The wood.'

Her knitting was on her lap, several rows pulled out, the wool in a tangle at her feet. I put the kettle on the stove intending to fill a flask.

'You're going back out?' she said.

I nodded. I felt tired and irritable.

'I can check on them.'

'You wouldn't know what to do if a lamb was coming.'

My tone, sharp, impatient. I winced. She came across to me and for a minute or more just stood behind me, silent, then I felt her hand on my back.

'Get a few hours sleep,' she said. 'You don't look well. I'll see it to it.'

'You'd panic out there alone.'

She withdrew her hand. 'I wouldn't.'

'You'd have to come and wake me and then it'd be too late.' I glared at her. 'We could lose another. And we can't, not one more.'

She stood dumbly, hands together, twisting her long, pale fingers. 'I know, Faye.'

'Do you? You think you do, but you don't know anything. We're up to our necks.'

I stared at the kettle, willing it to boil. I was angry and getting angrier. 'You were talking to Angus on the lane earlier, what about?'

'I don't remember.'

'Yes, you do. You were arguing. I saw you from the wood.'

'It was nothing.'

I looked at her, but she was avoiding my gaze. She took the flask, unscrewed the lid.

'*Clare?*'

'Honestly, Faye, I don't know what's got into you - except you must be exhausted. You're not yourself. We weren't arguing. We were talking about the shoot.'

Another lie. I covered my face with my hands, dragging my fingers down over my eyes.

'It'll be fine just as soon as lambing's over, Faye, you'll see.'

I thought of telling her I'd decided to accept Angus's offer of staying until lambing was over, but it'd only make matters worse between us and so I took the flask and went back out. A huge moon was beginning to find the shape of the barn, but the fields and copse were still bound to darkness. I settled on the straw beside the ewes and closed my eyes, but though I was tired and the darkness pulled and pulled, I couldn't drop off.

Outside, it'd begun to rain again, a tinny patter on the roof and, now and then, when the wind got hold of it, a wet slap. Hours later, when, finally, it stopped, it was eerily silent, several minutes before other sounds came back to me, and then, dumbly, like I was feeling for them: the snuffling of the sheep, the pad of their hooves on the straw, the cold, slow creep of water.

I lost two lambs that night, twins. The first was stillborn, but for hours it looked as though the second one would make it. After repeatedly putting it to the ewe, I'd given it what little milk it would accept and then fallen asleep with it in my arms. By morning, it was limp. I buried them both out the back of the stables, digging a hole in the earth beside the muckheap. Kneeling to cover them, I began to cry; angry heaving sobs that swallowed me like a giant wave. It was Angus who found me and took me, staggering, into the barn. Once I'd calmed down, he began to talk, whispering his plan softly in my ear, ignoring my protests. The fencing by the copse we'd do together, he'd fix the leaks in the barn roof next, sleep here, too, just until lambing was over. We'd shore up the ditch, perhaps even look to sell the old plough to raise money until market. By the time he left me, to go and finish clearing the oak, I'd agreed to all of it.

I went to the house to tell Clare, but met her on the yard. She was coming out with a tray of tea and toast.

'There you are. I brought you some breakfast.'

'I'm not hungry.'

She followed me into the kitchen, stood behind me as I pulled a blanket from the box in the closet.

'Were you cold? I should've fetched you a bottle.'

'It isn't for me. Angus is going to stay a few days. He'll sleep in the barn.'

The colour drained from her cheeks. She put down the tray on the table, pressed a hand again to her hip. 'Won't he be in your bed?'

I flung the blanket at her. It struck her face and dropped to the floor. Quietly, she picked it up and began to fold it. I turned away to the sink to wash the soil and blood off my hands. Why shouldn't I be angry?

Where'd *she* been all night? Tucked up in her bed, that's where. She didn't even know about the dead lambs, nor cared to know. But then how could she know? I'd have told her once.

'I hope you know what you're doing.' A sharp edge to her voice.

'We're not going to talk about this.'

'Don't I have a say?'

'It's decided. There are some things... It's farm business.'

'He'll betray you.' Her voice a wasp in my ear. 'First chance he gets.'

'He's just helping me with the lambing.'

'Aye and then what? He'll be offering to marry you next, you said you wanted to be married.'

'Look, I don't want to fight.' I dug into a blood-red cuticle with the edge of my thumbnail. 'He's here to help –'

'I can help you!' She paced behind me. 'You could show me things, but you won't. I think you want to suffer it alone; you want to make me feel bad so you can have Angus here.'

'You sound jealous.'

'Jealous? I don't want him.'

'Not *him.*'

A sharp intake of breath. So - it *was* true. It ought to have helped me understand, but I only felt my anger grow. Her love, yes, love - if that's what you could call it - felt like a trick. She moved away, sat in her chair, her back straight and tense.

'He wants to start a business here,' she said. 'Make a bed and breakfast out of the stables.'

'*What?*'

'You wanted to know what we were talking about on the lane so I'm telling you.'

'You said you were talking about the shoot.'

'That's what I *said.*'

'So you lied? What other lies have you told me?'

'None.'

I laughed. 'You didn't tell me about the woman who killed herself. Your *friend.*'

She glared at me.

'Did you love her, too?'

'Yes.'

I'd known it, but her admission was still a shock. Outside, the trill of a blackbird filled our silence. I sat down in the chair opposite her, gazing into the dead fire. 'Why did she kill herself?'

She was twisting her apron around her fingers.

'*Clare?*'

'She saw something.'

'What?'

'Something she wasn't supposed to see.' She closed her eyes. 'It drove her mad.'

'I don't understand.'

'He plays us off against each other, Faye. Angus. You don't see it, but he does.'

'*What did she see?*'

'We didn't used to be like this.'

I knelt in front of her. Her eyes were open now, wild looking. She wiped her cheeks and then held my face lightly in her hands. 'We were good, Faye.'

'*Tell me.*'

She was rocking softly now, pale, more fragile than I'd ever seen her. Suddenly, she clutched the sides of her head with both hands.

'It's all right. Don't upset yourself. I'll make you some tea.'

'No.' She rose to her feet, smoothing down her skirt. 'I think I'll just lie down.' At the door she looked back, but didn't quite meet my eyes, then, quietly, she made her way up the stairs.

I sat for a time, trying to make sense of it. What had the woman seen? What could be so bad that it'd make her go mad? Then, hearing Angus's voice outside, I put my boots on, not bothering to tie the laces, and went out onto the porch. The rain had slowed to a drizzle, but it was colder. Flint was pulling the fence planks through the gate into Well Field, Angus at his shoulder leading him. Something that involved Clare's father? I couldn't think of anything else, but Clare had only ever spoken of him kindly. Angus had been right. There were secrets. But did I really want to know what they were? To press her to talk about her past? Part of me wanted to forget it, just pretend nothing had happened for fear of something changing between us. I liked what we had, our simple life. It was love, what was between us was love. Did it matter what kind?

I stayed most of the day with the ewes while Angus repaired the fence. I could just as easily have left them for an hour - none showed signs of lambing - but Angus insisted, probably thinking it was as close to a rest as I'd ever agree to. And I did sleep a bit, only returning to the yard as light began to drain from the sky.

'We'll not be short of wood for the fire,' I said, as he piled up the last cuts of the oak. 'Come in and eat something now.'

'Might have a wash, then I'll go over the barn and fix that leak.'

'Tomorrow.'

'It's coming down onto your bales. You'll get mould, not good for the lambs.'

'All right then, but eat first.'

He placed a hand on my cheek. 'You look better.'

I waited while he scraped his boots and left them by the door and then, together, we went inside.

'You'll want to wash at the sink,' Clare said, tightly. 'I won't be a minute, just plating up.'

'I can go upstairs, save getting in your way,' Angus said. 'If I've time that is.'

She looked at him, at me. 'You've time.'

When he came down again, he'd changed his shirt; his hair wet and slicked back. 'Smells great.'

'Doesn't it?' I smiled at Clare. 'The flowers are nice too.'

'I got them from the wood.'

Angus took a seat at the head of the table and began tucking into his soup, dipping the bread and stuffing great mouthfuls in. 'I'll fix that leak and then stay out there tonight.'

'I'll come too,' I said.

'I'll call you if I need help.'

'Don't be silly. I couldn't let you –'

'He's offered hasn't he, Faye? What's the point of both of you being out there all night?'

Angus lifted the spoon to his mouth, curling his top lip back to save it burning. He cast a long slow look at Clare.

'Well, I'll help you with the leak at any rate,' I said. 'You'll be OK here, Clare?'

'Why wouldn't I be?' Her tone was sharp though she smiled quickly to soften it. 'I'll make you a flask, Angus. It'll be cold, you can take an extra blanket from the chest.'

He nodded, eating fast. Once he'd finished, he pushed his bowl out in front of him. 'Excuse me then. Clare, that was lovely. We'd better be making a start.'

I looked at her.

'Yes, yes. I'll clear up, off you go.' She rubbed the side of her face with her hand. 'I'll bring a flask out to you before I go to bed, then you can walk back with me if you're ready, Faye?'

'All right.'

Outside, Angus let out a long sigh. 'Well, that was awkward.'

'We had a bit of a spat earlier.'

'What about?'

'It doesn't matter.'

We crossed the yard into the barn and I sat on a bale while Angus inspected the leak. I'd dragged a trough under, but it was almost full and another hole had opened up farther along, rain dripping straight onto a hay round. The noise of it needled my brain. I could well imagine him telling Clare about his idea to turn the stables into a bed and breakfast. Other farmers had done it to supplement their income. I'd thought of doing it myself once, but I couldn't see a time when I'd ever have enough money. He'd only been trying to think up ways to help.

'Hey, you're shivering.' He took off his coat and put it across my shoulders and then sat beside me. 'I saw your stores, earlier when I went looking for the planks. Feed's low. Hay's down to –'

'You don't need to tell me.'

'So how long you got?'

'Weeks, maybe a month.'

'Does she know?'

'No. If I can just get the lambs to market I'll be in the clear.'

'Yeah, but you got to get them there. Fields are trashed, the ditch –'

'I know about the ditch, Angus.'

'I told you, didn't I?' He put his hands on my shoulders. 'We can do it, Faye, turn this place around. Oak's done, the fencing's done – that's two big jobs in as many days.'

'It's too much to ask.'

'There'll be no shoots here if I don't, it's in my own best interests.'

'I suppose.'

He put my hands around his waist. Perhaps it was easier to give in than to say no. The tips of his fingers found the skin under the hem of my blouse. I closed my eyes, let him kiss me, and then slowly, tentatively, I began to kiss him back. He pushed me down, dragging his lips and tongue down my neck. Yes, I'd wanted this, wanted it all along. It was how it was supposed to be. He undid the belt of my breeches, scrabbled with the buttons on his, his breath hot against my ear as he entered me, then his mouth was on mine again, smothering me, so urgent I could feel the jagged edge of his teeth pressing against my lips. Finally, his back arched and he let out a cry and rolled off me. I watched him do himself up, brushing hay off his shirt and then, grinning, he picked a strand from my hair. We lay back on the straw, my head on his chest.

'I better get back,' I said.

'Not yet.'

It was raining again, a light patter on the roof.

'I'll fetch you your flask at least.'

'No need.' Clare.

She stood at the door, the flask in her hand. She turned her head away as we stood up and then she cleared her throat and came inside. Her hair was dripping wet. Had she seen us? *Watched*? Angus looked angry, but he said nothing. He began moving bales so he could line up the ladder under the leak. Clare stood, tense, still, but her hands were trembling. Then, silently, she handed the flask to me and went out into the dark.

He was supposed to go once lambing was over and the last of the ewes had been turned away with their lambs, but there was no talk of it. Angus merely got on with the next job, and the next. I'd thought Clare would say something about it; I'd expected another row after she found us in the barn, but she didn't say a word and so we carried on, Angus and me on the farm, Clare going about her jobs as usual. It was only when, weeks later, I stood at the kitchen window watching her clear out the hen house, that I saw how much she'd changed. She still walked with the same awkward gait she'd had since her fall, but she was thinner, shrunken somehow, and with a nervous, hunted look that made me feel ashamed. It'd been easier to think she'd come to terms with things, that perhaps she understood how close we'd come to losing the farm and so had decided to put her own feelings to one side. But I could see now it wasn't true.

The morning of the shoot, Angus went off early to collect the shooting party from the station and I tried to clear the air. I found her in the kitchen scrubbing carrots.

'Can I help?' I asked.

'Nothing to do really.'

'I could prepare the slaw.'

She placed the carrots on the chopping board. 'You can finish these, if you like.'

I sat at the table, Clare with her back to me. She pulled over a bag of potatoes and started to peel them over the sink.

'You should know I've decided to take a place in Murton,' she said.

'A place?'

'A room, it isn't much.'

I opened my mouth to speak, I'd not foreseen this. Not her *leaving*. 'Don't be silly, you can't –'

'It's decided. I've paid the deposit.'

'No!' I stood up, pulled her round to face me. Her face was bone-white, the skin beneath her eyes so dark it looked almost purple. 'I know things haven't been great, but Angus is leaving, it just made sense for him to stay until –'

'It isn't because of Angus.'

I stared at her.

'Oh God, Faye, I don't want a fuss, please don't make this hard. I was always going to see you through the shoot, but I must go.'

'Sod the bloody shoot!'

'I can't bear to be here any longer, I just can't!'

'Please, Clare. I need you.'

'You have Angus.'

'So it *is* him. I know you think he wants to marry me and –'

'No, it's not him, it's us.' She shook her head. 'Me. I thought when I found this place and you... God it's so *stupid*.'

'What is?'

'I thought it'd be forever.'

'It can be. *This* is your home.'

She pressed her fingers into her eyes. 'I've been such a fool, Faye.'

'You haven't, you –'

'I thought if I loved you enough....' She smudged tears from her cheeks with the heel of one hand. 'But it can't happen again. I won't let it.'

'What can't happen again?'

I heard Angus's car pull on to the yard. Voices. Max started growling.

'What? Tell me.'

'Go. He'll expect you to greet them.'

95

'*Clare.*'

'Go, go on, they'll want their flasks.'

'All right, but after they've gone then, we'll talk. Promise me?'

The door swung open and Angus put his head round. 'There you are, they're here.' A black Labrador was nuzzling between his knees, trying to get into the kitchen much to the annoyance of Max. 'Get him locked up, will you?'

'Max!'

'C'mon, we'll need to get a move on to make the most of the weather.'

I grabbed Max's collar and dragged him, barking, into the washroom, then followed Angus out onto the yard. More dogs were spilling out the backs of trucks. Angus brought the men together to begin the safety briefing. Some of the faces I recognized from earlier shoots, but there were several new ones and a young boy, small, his hair cropped short in the same style as his father who stood beside him, a hand on his shoulder. He'd be no more than fourteen. A few were still getting their kit together, but then gradually the talking and laughing subsided and there was just Angus's voice. When he'd finished, they lined up to take their flasks from me; several had brought their own, but they took ours as well. When the young lad took his there was a cheer.

'We'll come back through Bankfoot as usual,' Angus said, lifting his gun bag onto his shoulder. 'About 2pm I should think, unless it's good over Bracken Hill then it'll be more like four.'

I nodded. 'We'll have everything ready.'

He kissed me on the cheek and then set off, leading the group up Hill Field. I watched them until they disappeared into the wood and then went into the kitchen to find Clare. A large pot was simmering away on the stove, but there was no sign of her. I checked the sitting room and then went upstairs, finding her door closed. A single shot rang out, an early rabbit for someone. I knocked and went inside, but the room was empty. Then, through the window, I saw her, her shawl and blue velvet cap, a shopping bag over her arm, though I don't know why; we already had everything we needed.

When she returned, two hours later, she slipped quietly into the farmhouse to set the table. Everything was ready by three o'clock, but at four-thirty the shoot still hadn't returned. I was starting to get worried, I kept looking for them coming over the rise behind the wood. The light was fading fast.

'I think I'll go up on the top, see if I can see them from the edge of Bankfoot,' I told her.

'That rabbit'll be tender,' Clare said.

'Won't it just!' I took the lamp from the closet and went to the window.

'You don't think there's been an accident?'

'What, like they're so drunk they've shot each other instead of the deer?'

'Don't joke, Faye.'

'They'll be drunk enough. Half of them had their own flasks, didn't stop them taking ours.'

'Be careful.' She touched my arm. 'You won't go beyond the wood, will you?'

I stepped out onto the porch and turned on the lamp, wanting, more than anything, to stay by the fire with Clare and talk, but it was right to get the shoot over with first. The field was slippy underfoot and it took me a lot longer than usual to reach the edge of Bankfoot. I looked for the pond to find my bearings, straight on past that and I'd see the rise and could look for them on the moorland path. A flash of something in the light of the lamp. The pond. Toads. Dozens of them. Two males and a female in a mating ball. A body of another female lying bloated and lifeless on her back.

I pushed on to the rise, searching for the beams of lamps, listening for the dogs, but there was only darkness and silence. I turned left along the top edge of Bankfoot until I reached the path that led down the side of Harrison's land. The field, red raw for months, now had a skin of green. Then, out of the corner of my eye, I glimpsed lights, swinging left and right, heard voices. That was them. Had to be. I waited, saw two men supporting another man under each arm. Drunk? No. *Injured.*

'Faye?'

I lowered the lamp. 'What's wrong?'

'Oh, he'll live, won't you, Tommy? Fell down a ravine, took four of us to get him out.'

Tommy waved a hand at me, lost his balance, and all three men staggered into the group to their left.

'He's drunk,' I said.

'Whisky's kept the edge off the pain. They're starving, mind. Go ahead, Craig, you know the way now, right?' He turned back to me.

'What's with you coming looking for us?'

'You said four. I was worried.'

'Sure sign you're falling for me, that is.'

Some of the men laughed. He was drunk, too, slurring his words - they all were. Singing their heads off as they moved down through the wood.

'You shouldn't let them drink like that. No wonder he fell down a ravine.'

'What's got you in a mood? Clare bitching about us not being back? Hey, we only got a *stag*.' He leaned into me. 'They'll come in droves now. Jamie - he's the one who got it - says he'll come back next year with his clients, rich property man he is, owns half bloody Kent.'

I watched them filing through the trees, stumbling over fallen branches, cheering. 'Well, they'll not keep coming if one of them gets shot.'

He jabbed me hard in the shoulder. 'Look, I run the shoots, you do the food. We show them a good time, that's it. Good for you, good for me.'

He strode ahead, catching up with the rest of them and joining in with their shouts and laughter. I followed behind only catching up when we were back on the yard. It'd shocked me seeing that flash of temper, not that I knew he didn't have one, but he'd not turned it on me before. It was the drink, I thought, and hurried forward to help Angus take the injured man through to the sitting room while the others took off their boots.

'Sit yourself down there, Tommy lad. I'll get Clare, she'll soon patch you up.'

'No, I'll do it. Clare's busy with the food.'

Angus shrugged. Clare appeared at the doorway. 'What on earth's happened?'

'Two women fussing over you now, Tommy, eh?'

Tommy gave him a thumbs up and Clare and Angus went into the kitchen.

'I'll take your boot off, OK, Tom?' I said. 'Sorry if it hurts.'

'I can't feel it much, only when I walk on it.' His eyes lowered to my chest. 'You and him together then?'

'No.'

'You're pretty.'

I unrolled the bandage onto his ankle.

'Sorry, girls in the office are all up themselves.'

'I think you should have a doctor look at this.'

'A'be all right. Lenny'll drop me back at my lodgings later.'

I glanced at the hip flask in his hand, at the wedding ring on his finger. 'Back in a minute.'

I went to find Angus; he was slapping James' back and they were all singing, *'For he's a jolly good fellow.'*

'Angus?'

He was laughing, swigging whisky from a mug. Clare was dishing out food, but only a few of the men and the young lad had sat down to eat, the rest were keener on drinking, helping themselves to the brandy she'd put out for after the meal.

'Angus?' I pulled his arm, he turned. 'Tom needs a doctor.'

'And so say all us! And so say all of us!'

'He's fine, give him a drink.'

'N-o, I think he's broken something.'

He turned to face me, steadying himself on my shoulder. 'He's not asking for a doctor, is he?'

'He's too drunk to know any better.'

'Jesus, Faye, what's got into you?'

'We're supposed to be looking after everybody. My job –'

'Your job's to make sure the only memories Tommy goes home with are of having a bloody good time with the boys, not spending the last few hours of his jolly fannying over a sprained ankle.'

I shrugged his arm off my shoulder. 'I'm taking him.'

'Patch him up and give him a drink. You need to be here.'

'Clare can cope while I'm gone.'

'No, she can't. She's bloody useless.' He pulled me closer, his voice thinned to a hiss. 'You see that guy over there?' He pointed at James. 'He's just shot a *stag*. His cock's so fucking hard you could hang your coat off it. And what he wants to be doing is bragging about it to a pretty girl, not that dried up old cow.'

I looked at Clare. She was jumpy, frantic, trying to do a million things at once. One of the men asked her something, smiling at her, but she couldn't concentrate on what he was saying. Thinking he wanted more food she put another bowl in front of him, which clearly wasn't what he was asking. He looked at his friend and laughed.

Angus shoved me towards James, but I pushed him back. 'You pay for the food, you don't pay for me!'

I went over to help Clare, feeling Angus's steady glare follow me around the room. Now and then I turned; saw him filling his mug or else watching me, looking angrier all the time. I made sure everyone got a plate and then, gradually, with hot food inside them, the need to sleep overtook the need to drink and the group began to thin out until, finally, there was only four or five in the kitchen and Angus and another man on the porch. A gun shot, laughter. I went outside.

Angus was smothering a grin. 'Ah, Faye. Thought I saw your fox.'

'I need not remind you of the lambs,' I said.

He looked sheepishly at the other man and they laughed. When I went back inside, the remaining men were gathering up their coats, thanking Clare for the food. Dogs, tails wagging, rose from the rug by the fire. The boy, who'd fallen asleep with his head on the table, was shaken awake by his father and led out.

Tommy appeared from the sitting room, several degrees more sober than he'd been earlier. 'Thanks for patching me up, Faye. I appreciate it. See you next time.'

'Make sure you go to the doctor and have that checked out.'

'I'll be sure to, thanks for having us then. Lenny out there is he? And Angus?'

'Yes.'

He limped outside, shook Angus's hand and then left with Lenny. After a few minutes, Angus came into the kitchen, staggered and fell into an armchair. Clare looked at the dishes but started packing bottles into an empty box instead.

'It'll wait 'till morning, Clare,' I said. 'Get yourself up to bed. I'm going out to do the checks.'

'Aye, them lambs'll be startled, Faye,' Angus mumbled.

Outside, the moon was near full, a sulpherous halo around it. The cold edge of the wind found my bare neck and I shivered. Angus was a rotten drunk and I'd been a fool to sleep with him. He was too drunk to drive or I'd have sent him on his way now. Be too much of a job getting him to the barn, but he'd sleep it off in the chair and then, in the morning, I'd make sure he went. The lambs were skittish, more so than usual, but otherwise fine. Angus had been lucky with those men. Next time there'd be an accident, a serious one, and I wanted no part in it.

I walked back to the farmhouse, but before I'd got halfway there, I heard a commotion in the kitchen. A clatter, like a chair falling over, and then a smash. I ran the last few steps and flung the door open.

Angus was on the kitchen table, face down. My first thought was that, in his drunken fog, he was trying to climb on top of it to sleep, but then I realized Clare was underneath him, her skirt bunched up round her thighs. I blinked, my heart erupting into my throat. Had the two of them really been together all along, carrying on right under my nose? But then, *no...* Clare let out a scream. He put a hand over her mouth, yelped when she bit him. Her eyes were bulging, legs kicking out. She screamed again.

DO something.

I grabbed his shirt with both hands and hauled him back. A flash of the tops of Clare's white thighs and running down one of them, a pink scar. A second when Clare's eyes met mine, then Angus rolled over, fell off the table and crashed onto the floor. For a few moments he was still and so I pulled Clare up, but then he was on his knees, looking around him. Seeing me, he growled and lunged, swiping a chair out of his way. I grabbed a pan off the stove, but I wasn't quick enough and I felt his hands close around my throat. I fell to the floor, Angus on top of me, pressing down. I fought for a breath, felt tears stream from my eyes. He was astride me now, teeth bared.

Clare, a blur. She was behind him, clawing at his head and shoulders. She managed to get him to release me long enough so I could take a breath. I looked for the pan, snatched it up and waved it blindly until, finally, I felt it make contact. I brought it down again in the same place and his body went limp. I pushed him off, wriggling out from under him. Blood. On his head, on the floor. I'd hit him on side of his head, just above the ear. I sat, breathless, panting, clutching my throat. Clare knelt beside me. She was muttering, no words I could make out. I stared at Angus, his bare arse was poking out the back of his trousers.

Clare. Her eyes were wild, her mouth open as if in a scream, but she was silent. I reached for her hand and pulled her into an embrace, her hot, wet cheek against mine.

'Oh Clare, I'm sorry.'

Angus was groaning, but quite still. We had to get out, get the police. Think, *think*. I'd lock him in the washroom. Keep him there until it they arrived.

I pulled Clare's hands free of mine, but she clung to me.

'Just for a minute. I'm not going far, I promise.'

I stood up, coughing, dizzy, but managed to take Angus by the ankles and drag him to the washroom. Once there, he rolled over, groaning again, but made no attempt to get up. Key. *Key?* Where was it? I looked for it on the hook beside the door, but then remembered I'd left it in the sitting room when I fetched the first aid kit for Tommy. I grabbed it from the coffee table and raced back to the kitchen. My hands were shaking so much it took several attempts to lock the door, but then, yes, locked. I put a chair under the handle for good measure.

Clare. She wasn't where I'd left her, just her shawl lying in a knot on the floor, crumpled and blood stained. 'Clare?'

I looked in the sitting room, though I knew she couldn't be there, then in the bedrooms. She had to be outside. The light was starting to thin, nothing moving, nothing stirring. I checked the barn, calling her all the time, then ran to the stables, all the places I thought she might hide, and then I searched the house again. Finally, exhausted, I returned to the kitchen.

A sour, feral smell seemed to have gathered there in my absence. She'd gone. Confused, I slumped into a chair, not knowing where else to search. Gone. There was only her painting, filling the wall above the hearth, the hare poised in the act of leaping into the room.

She didn't return that night, or the next. Some weeks later, when the sheep had no daily need of me, I set to work to search for her. First, I went to Murton where I tracked down the room she'd paid the deposit on, but the landlady said she'd never moved in. Then I went to the farmhouse in Leigh where Clare had lived with her father and the woman. Sarah. It had been easy enough to find her name; the Leigh advertiser had a front-page story about it – suicide in local quarry. A history of mental illness, the coroner said. But there'd been more to it than that, I knew.

She saw something she wasn't supposed to see.

I was haunted by the life Clare had lived before she met me, and by her quiet, loving presence. The songs she played in the evenings in winter; the scar on her thigh. I see that scar whenever I close my eyes. Even now, a year on, I hear her moving around upstairs, feel her in the kitchen sitting by the fire. It makes no sense, but it comforts me. I suppose I'm still waiting for her to come home.

The hares remind me of her, and every day I take a while to watch them. They've done well this year; their numbers have grown. I'm beginning to be able to tell them apart. There's one who has an especially gawky appearance, ungainly. I wonder whether it's the hare I found trapped in the wire as she moves as though one leg is a little weaker. I watch her now, being pursued by a jack. She turns, rises up into the air, kicks out a punch with her hind legs, and then she races on.

On my lap, Max shivers and showers me with a mist of raindrops. Each downpour's scarcely over before the next arrives, fat-bellied clouds chivied along by the wind in an apparently endless line. I am never far from rain ●